A Joe LaFlam Mystery

MY FEAR LADY

aka The Case of Twelve

RICK DEWHURST

Quotidian Books
Duncan, BC

Published by Quotidian Books
Duncan, BC
Printed in Charleston, SC

ISBN: 0-9867457-0-7
ISBN-13: 978-0-9867457-0-6
Library of Congress Control Number: 2010904633

For Mom, Dad, and sister Bonnie

CHAPTER ONE

The rain hammered down outside my penthouse office by the sea. It nailed the converted and the unconverted alike. The rain knew no distinctions. You could be an archbishop or a pedophile, a taxi driver or a Christian detective, the rain didn't care. No matter who you were, when the wet stuff came down, down it came, and all that mattered was whether or not you were wearing a hat, or whether or not you had an umbrella, or whether or not you had a roof over your head. It didn't have to be a fancy roof like mine, a big-city penthouse roof in the Pacific Northwest, where you not only stayed dry, you lived well. It might just be a roof; one that didn't leak, or maybe it only leaked in a few places, like in the old days when you were tortured by the monotonous drops plunking into aluminum cooking pots, drowning out the television.

My intercom buzzed my thoughts.

"Send them in," I said.

"There's nobody here," Pen said.

"What then?"

"You don't have to take that attitude."

"Fine. What's up?" I said.

"Lunch, I'll be back later," she said.

"Okay, I'll mind the store."

My secretary Penelope was a good kid, a stepsister who'd needed something to do while she was finding herself, and then there was the pressure from the family. They were paying the bills.

My intercom buzzed again. I clicked.

"Are you there?" It was a seductive female voice, hanging unclad in my office's warm air.

"I'm here," I said, sitting up in my chair.

The door opened and in she slithered, right across the carpet— my rich, big-city carpet that belonged in a big-city detective's office like mine—and then she slid into my affluent detective's chair in front of my big mahogany detective's desk. She was built like Cher in her Sonny days. Her hair was long and black and shiny and straight, like it had been flattened by a road crew in the heat of summer. She didn't scare me a bit. I looked her straight in the eye, and then I looked her straight in the other one. She had two yellow ones, each placed on either side of her dagger nose. I'd never seen yellow eyes before. I had a hunch they were fake. I tried not to look intrigued.

"You got yellow eyes," I said.

"Smooth talker," she said.

"You don't scare me a bit," I said.

"Too bad, I was trying to."

Her wit was sharp. So was her nose, but it gave her character. It was the kind of nose I could live with, in a pinch, but to live with it for the long haul, well, it would have to be God.

"Who knows?" I said. My thoughtless words paused to determine their effect and then, disowned, faded away. I assumed a reflective pose and stared above her nose and over her head, my eyes searching for escape in the white of the eggshell ceiling.

"Who knows what?" she said.

"Good question," I said. I decided to take another tack. "So what brings you into my penthouse detective's office?"

"That's easy. The Yellow Pages say you're a Christian detective and..." Her story skipped a beat as she slipped into vocal introspection, continuing as if I wasn't there. She said, "I've lost the ability to trust, and I thought that a Christian detective would be trustworthy, if you know what I mean. And I really do need a detective." She then redirected her soliloquy to the wall over my left shoulder. "You are trustworthy, aren't you?" The wall had nothing to say. Her now vulnerable, yellow eyes, set beneath her sharp, indelible brow, darted from the mute wall to rest on my sternum, where they pleaded with my mid-section to be her hero. I wouldn't let her down.

"I think so," I said.

"Excellent, that's all I wanted to hear."

"So what's the scoop?" I said.

"Have you ever heard of Spelunkers Global?"

Sure. It figured. I felt that old feeling in the back of my neck, the one that says you'd better pay attention or you'll be dead meat, no matter how you sliced it. Not that I was ever going to be dead meat, or at least I didn't think I was ever going to be, since nobody ever died in my cases.

One thing was for certain. Spelunkers Global were pulling my chain, and they'd sent this slick smart-cracker to bait me. Did she think I was born yesterday? Her yellow eyes could see I was in my early thirties, none the worse for wear and physically fit, despite the fast food. My dark brown hair—some even said it was black— had playful curls. The blue eyes were an asset. Six feet tall. Sturdy. I'd heard some women say I was cute, others, handsome. A little paunch, but so what. But would I ever marry?

It seemed to me that a long time had passed between her last question about the Spelunkers and my immediate reply.

"I'm wise to you, Princess," I said.

"Wise? I really don't know if you're...oh, I see. Well, I guess what really counts is whether or not you're a good detective. That's the main thing."

"Fair enough," I said. "So let's hear it."

"Hear what?"

"Your sad story," I said.

"Am I that obvious?"

"Sure, but that never stops me."

Then I heard it, a purring sound, and it was coming from her. What a day!

Her purring paused, and she said, "I got mixed up with this guy who said he'd give me the world, and then he didn't."

Her purr then convulsed, and a tear dripped from the corner of one yellow eye. The other eye looked on, unaffected.

"All he left me were memories," she said.

"Memories?"

"Yes, memories. We were engaged and…and…then he fell for one of those Spelunkers, and the two of them went underground, leaving me high and dry."

So, he was a fallen man, and she was a fallen woman. But I wasn't the one to pass judgment. Who was I? But whoever I was, I was starting to warm up to her. A little plastic surgery, or not. No big deal. But her looks were irrelevant when it came to the job. I was a professional, and she needed the services of Joe LaFlam, Christian Detective. And Spelunkers or no Spelunkers, I was her man.

"Two hundred a day, plus expenses," I said.

"I haven't even told you what I want you to do yet."

"It doesn't matter, when I make up my mind, I make up my mind."

"A little steep."

"How about a hundred?"

What difference did the money make? I was loaded. What I needed was a case, a case that mattered, one that would make my life a better place to be.

She nodded her agreement to my counter offer. The die was cast. Spelunkers Global were on the prowl again, and I was ready to stare my fear in the face. What did I have to lose?

"I want you to find my Jake," she said. "He's just a little mixed up right now. She's no good for him. What kind of life is that? Hiding out in caves."

"Spelunking's no life at all," I said.

"You are wise," she said, tossing me a bone.

"You didn't tell me your name," I said.

"Sissy, Sissy Smith."

"You don't look like a Sissy."

"Everyone says that."

"Have you got a picture?"

"Of? Oh, you mean Jake, yes, right here."

She slipped a slender hand into her purse and produced a Polaroid. "There."

She handed me Jake and her, captured on film in happier days. He had a Kung Fu moustache. I guessed Sissy was about 5'7", and Jake was about a foot taller.

"He's kind of tall for a cave dweller, isn't he?" I said.

"He's not a natural. Spelunking's just not him. That's what I mean. She's no good for him either."

I gave her back the Polaroid. She returned it to her bag, took out a black handkerchief, and gave her dagger a blow. What's in a nose? I thought. A nose by any other name would smell as sweet. I knew that plastic surgeons were doing a booming business in the Church these days. Many with prophetic gifts were paying for nose jobs, so they could look more like eagles.

"There's something else," she said.

"My expenses?"

"No, your expenses are fine. What I mean is, I think something bad might have happened to Jake."

"Bad? What could be worse than living underground?"

"No, you don't understand. I think they might have, you know, it's hard to say out loud."

"Killed him?"

"Oh, don't say it!"

"Why would they kill him?"

"The witch who stole Jake is the daughter of one of the World Rulers. Jake wouldn't be good enough for her. They wouldn't let him out either, do you see?"

"Leave it to me. If he's alive, if they haven't killed him, I'll bring him up. That's what they pay me for. Last name?"

"I told you, it's Smith. Oh, you mean Jake. It's Dano, Jake Dano."

The door opened and in came my two partners, Alfred and Abner, bickering. Abner was keeping up his end of the argument, while shoving the last of a sub sandwich into his mouth.

"Ya know as well as I do," Abner said, "Nixon sold the country out takin' the dollar off the gold standard."

"You don't have all the facts," Alfred said, and took a superior drag on his bottled water. In his mid-fifties, Alfred was aging well. Only a few lines of grey streaked his slicked-back, black hair. And despite a few extra pounds, he looked distinguished and durable in his black suit.

"I got enough facts to know...," Abner said. He stopped talking, chewing, and walking. He'd spotted black-haired Sissy with the yellow eyes sitting in our client's chair. He scratched his sandy-grey hair and then pointed his stubbly red-leather face at Sissy.

"Who are you?" Abner said.

"This is Sissy," I said.

"Ya don't look like a Sissy," Abner said. "Ain't never seen a Sissy with yellow eyes before neither."

"Don't be rude," Alfred said.

"This is Abner Bell and Alfred Booker," I said, "they're my partners." And then to lighten the mood, I added, "Bell, Booker, and LaFlam, at your service."

"Charmed," she said, "but I can't pay for three."

"No extra charge," I said, "we're a team."

Abner and Alfred pulled up a couple of chairs.

"So what have we got here?" Alfred said.

"Sissy's been jilted by Spelunkers," I said.

Alfred sat straight up in his chair.

"Spelunkers?" he said. "It can't be."

"Get real," Abner said, burping turkey.

"So, these men work for you?" Sissy said. She turned up her nose to accentuate her point.

"Like three peas in a pod," Abner said. "Can't ya tell?"

Alfred cleared his throat and glared at Sissy.

"Are you a Spelunker?" he said.

Sissy, the black-haired slinker with the sharp nose, looked at me with her yellow cat's eyes and then turned to Alfred.

"Who wants to know?" she said.

"Well, are you?" Alfred said.

"Go easy," I said.

Then, Sissy, who really didn't look like a Sissy, said, "Spelunkers are the lowest form of animal."

I could see she wasn't going to answer, so I decided to move the conversation along.

"We might as well tackle them head on," I said. "What have we got to lose?"

"Our lives?" Alfred said.

"Well, I ain't got no pension comin' so it don't matter to me," Abner said.

I decided not to tell Alfred nobody ever died in my cases. Why would I spoil the fun? And besides, I wasn't lead-pipe positive it was the truth. Alfred gave Sissy the once-over, once more.

"Are you sure you're not one of them?" he said.

Sissy looked to me for support. I didn't have any to give. I didn't care whether she was one of them or not, even though it seemed to matter to Alfred. I was beyond caring who was who when it came to the Spelunkers. The only thing I knew was that they had to be exposed. Light had to be shone down every stinking gopher hole they'd burrowed themselves into. It was the case of the century and of the millennium. And it had fallen into my lap again. Sure, I knew they were feeling me out to see what I would do next. They were drawing me in to measure me up and plant me in that old pine box six-feet under, where they could keep a closer eye on me. And sure, it was a setup, but I'd been set up before. Setups were nothing new to me, and Sissy was a dead giveaway. So why hadn't they sent someone more convincing? I might have been insulted, if I cared what the Spelunkers thought of me. No, it didn't matter anymore. What would your average citizen have done, knowing there was a conspiracy among all the power brokers in the world, to bring the population into the slavery of a one-world government, ruled by a corrupt elite, whose only goal was more—more for them—while they peddled the people of the western world the lie that illicit sex and drugs and reality TV were good for them? And for the have-nots in the rest of the downtrodden world, they promised the redistribution of wealth, so the have-nots could get their fair share of sex and drugs, too, and hooray for Hollywood? Some people would have just changed the channel, but I wasn't made that way. I had to get the goods on them, or die trying, though it was highly unlikely I would die in my own case, since there wouldn't be anybody left to tell the story, and then the end of the case would never be known. But if it did turn out there was no end to the story, that would mean I'd met my end, and that the Spelunkers of the earth had won. Joe LaFlam, alive no more, and the world subjected to the cruel slavery of the diabolical Underlords, who would have by then emerged as Overlords. I was the only one who stood in their way. And I wouldn't let the world down.

My reverie ended, I nodded at Alfred. A nerve twitched in my eyelid that forced a wink. Sissy didn't notice.

"Ya got somethin' in your eye?" Abner said.

Sissy began to purr again. Abner stuck a finger in his ear, wiggled it in there, shook his head, and looked at Sissy.

"So ya got the breathin' problems?" Abner said. "Too bad, a young person like yerself."

Sissy choked at Abner's concern, and then coughed, but the expected hairball failed to show.

"So, you've been jilted by Spelunkers?" Alfred said.

Sissy began to sob on cue.

"My man, Jake," she said. "I love my Jake, but he was seduced by a Spelunker female and taken underground. You...you...have to find him."

Alfred was unimpressed with Sissy's performance and sat back in his chair.

"I ain't goin' into no cave," Abner said. "Can't stand bein' closed in. I couldn't have been more than eight, kid next door locked me in his sister's hope chest. Wouldn't let me out till I promised to marry 'er."

"We've got to help her," I said to Alfred.

Abner said, "As long as I don't have to crawl around in some cave."

"Okay, fine," Alfred said. "Why not take the plunge? There's no sense in trying to avoid the inevitable."

"We're all in?" I said.

Alfred nodded, and then Abner said, "Ya, ya, one fer all and all fer one; let's just get started."

Sissy purred some more.

She was interesting, but was that enough? And why was I always drawn to these unusual dames? It was almost as if they'd been put on the planet as a test. And was I being tested again? And, if so, would I pass this time, or fail? I'd never passed in the past, and what would passing be like? I might never know. But that was a negative attitude. I needed to make a habit of speaking positive words into my own life, but, since I was thinking right now, I really meant I should think positive words. This was either the beginning of a beautiful friendship, one that would continue to blossom into eternity, or just one more tragic case of deceit and betrayal. Knowing the human race as I did—and what gumshoe didn't—I figured the odds at five-to-one for the latter, though, of course, as a Christian, I never bet on horses, or even went to the track. And then it hit me again. Thinking positive thoughts was hard.

"We need to get a few more details," I said to Sissy.

"Certainly," she said. "I would be happy to answer any additional questions you might have. And be assured, I am very grateful you are taking the case."

"That's why we get out of bed in the morning," I said.

"I hardly sleep at all anymore," Abner said. "At least two or three trips a night now."

A somber Alfred said, "There's a good chance we'll all end up dead."

I ignored Alfred's negativity and tried to remember. Were the stalactites on the bottom or top? I was pretty sure from high school science class that the stalagmites were on the bottom and the stalactites on top. "Stalactite" even sounded more like one of those sharp rock icicles, and "stalagmites" sounded more like cow pies.

"It don't really matter one way or the other," Abner said, nodding at the rest of us, "ever'body ends up dead anyway."

CHAPTER TWO

I sat on the living room sofa, reflecting on the day's events. Who was this Sissy Smith, that was the question, and what was her game? Maybe I should have asked her out, not on a client-detective basis, but on a date-basis. Who knew? I thumbed the clicker at the box and flashed up CNN. Trouble as usual. Protesters were tossing rocks at the riot police and chanting slogans outside a conference center where high-ranking Globalists were meeting. Tear gas was the response. The protesters' hearts were in the right place, but they were naive. Nobody had bothered telling them that the trouble wasn't up here but down there. The Spelunkers kept that dirty little secret hidden below. To them, the protesters were irrelevant. What did they care? When the time came, up the rulers would pop, and the anti-Globalists would either see things their way or be removed from the human equation. I clicked to another news channel, and then to another, to absorb the ever-unfolding mosaic of the world's news.

"Would you please stop?" Aunt Margaret said. "All that clicking around turns my stomach."

"Sorry."

I thanked God for my Aunt Margaret. When I'd discovered my new family, and that she wasn't my real mother but my aunt, she had been kind enough to allow me a grace period while I adjusted. There had been no point in moving, no point in living on my own during such a traumatic change in my life. Sure, I could have decided to share a place with Alfred and Abner, but why, when Aunt

Margaret was happy to let me stay? The other option was to move in with my new family, but that would have posed relationship challenges, especially with my new sisters. And I wasn't prepared right now to tackle the job of developing relationships with my new parents either. I was safer here with Aunt Margaret, and the proper time to move out was when I found the future Mrs. LaFlam. The best plan was for my family and me to develop our relationships from a distance, and later, with a bride at my side, we wouldn't have to get too close.

"Put on the *Jeopardy*, dear," Aunt Margaret said. "It helps to keep my mind sharp."

"It's not on now. Comes on later in the evening."

"No need to be grouchy."

"I'm not grouchy. I'm just telling you the facts."

Aunt Margaret shifted her eyes from the TV to me.

"Yes, maybe I did fail," she said, "not telling you the facts of life sooner, and, you know, not telling you about...."

"Don't start again. I've got a new life now, and I'm rich. I've got no worries. Forget the past."

"I'm really not suggesting you're in denial," she said.

"Not that again."

"And I'm not saying you're passive-aggressive, either. I just think you might want to take a good look at your priorities."

My former mom, now my aunt, had never majored in encouragement. But I'd known her long enough to realize that she only used her sharp tongue to defend her soft heart. Her long, brown, straw hair, parted in the middle, framed a once-beautiful face, and in the opinion of Alfred and Abner, whose comments I'd overheard, Aunt Margaret had indeed kept her figure also.

"Don't look at me like that," she continued, "I'm just trying to help. Oh, hold on, it's *The Price is Right*."

Aunt Margaret lost herself in the cost of things, and I left her there.

In my room, there was space to think. I lay on my bed, the bed I'd grown up on, the bed that knew me better than I did, and I thought about what former-mom, now my aunt, had said. Sure, I had a tendency to be a dreamer, but there was no way I was in denial. Reality was a detective's stock and trade. A private detective had to stay in touch. But my spiritual life was a different story these days. It wasn't pretty. We all knew the pattern. First, you don't even open the cover of the Book most days, and praying, well there's no time, and then you skip a Sunday or two—with legitimate excuses—at least you tell yourself they're legitimate, and then next, well, it gets worse after that. I needed a spiritual turnaround, especially for the sake of Alfred and Abner. A back-slidden mentor was no mentor at all. But how was I to get back on that sharp spiritual edge? There were spiritual disciplines I might try. Martyrdom was the most effective, but it was self-defeating as far as the mentoring process was concerned. The next most powerful was celibacy, and then there was fasting and prayer, and then prayer alone. All were spiritual sacrifices, and all had their good points. I knew for sure I wasn't called to martyrdom; besides, martyrdom was something you had to work at. Fasting was out. It had its good points, but overall, denying yourself food had its down side. Sure, fasting killed the sex drive, and that was a blessing, but at what cost? Torment, mostly. And going without food was just plain unnatural. That left celibacy. It was hard to look at, but maybe that was the answer, since I was down on my luck in the mating game anyway, though as a Christian I wasn't supposed to believe in luck. Sure, maybe celibacy was the answer. I was called to a life of abstinence and had been just too stubborn to see it. What else might have accounted for my slack performance over the years? Maybe it was time to face it. Women weren't drawn to me for some reason, despite my natural good looks. My path had been pre-ordained. I was destined to live a life of spouse-less sacrifice. I would be an excellent example for Alfred and Abner, who were tripping over each other in their pursuit of

my Aunt Margaret. And, as everyone knew, celibacy had the potential to release loads of spiritual power. Sure, problem solved; there
would be power galore to solve Sissy's case, and in the process take
care of the Spelunkers once and for all. The world saved, and all due
to the selfless, sacrificial life of Joe LaFlam, who gave up the mating
game for the sake of others. It was something to think about. I'd
show Alfred and Aunt Margaret who was in denial and who wasn't.
I decided to marry my thoughts with some immediate action. I left
my room.

"I'm going out," I shouted to Aunt Margaret.

"Don't be long, dear. Remember you need to take time for dinner before your meeting tonight."

I piled into my Mercedes and headed down Fifth Street. I had
no particular direction in mind. I liked to think and drive. It was
relaxing. I remembered my taxi driving days, when I needed the
extra dough to keep my shingle hanging outside my former small-
time office on the hand-to-mouth side of town. No more of those
poverty days for me. But I liked to remember those times, because
if you didn't remember them, you were destined to repeat them,
or something like that. But my life history was a simple tale com-
pared to the life of the world. The world was a fine place to be if
you didn't know any better. But if you did, the trouble began. And
the Spelunker trouble began for me that night when I discovered
the briefcase left in my taxi by Alfred, then a Spelunker hit-man,
who was now my partner, Alfred Booker. The briefcase contained
the whole lowdown on the Spelunker conspiracy. And that's when
the trouble started, but that's also when I began the trip down the
road to easy street and my new rich family. Ironic. You had to take
the good with the bad in this life.

I wasn't in the mood to go back home and join Aunt Margaret
for dinner, which meant I had some time to kill before homegroup.
I grabbed my headset and beeped her number.

"I'm not coming home for dinner," I said.

"You might have told me sooner, dear. I've told you before, you need to be more considerate. If you ever get married, she might not turn out to be as understanding as I am, dear. They seldom are."

"Okay, I'm sorry. I should have told you before you started making dinner."

"Oh, I haven't started making it yet, dear."

"See you after homegroup," I said.

"That group hasn't helped you grow much, has it, dear?"

"Thanks, bye."

Sure, that was fine. She was entitled to her opinion. But right now I needed some food. I saw the Golden Arches and pulled in. Money hadn't spoiled me. I still enjoyed the meal of the masses.

CHAPTER THREE

Homegroup began at 7:30. The first half hour was taken up with refreshments. Two jelly donuts and a cola at the snack table topped off my earlier Quarter Pounder meal. I was settled and ready for the evening's journey into faith, growth, and fellowship. Seated in the living room, I looked around at my group mates, the ones I'd chosen to share my life with. I was thankful we were a small group. Conventional church wisdom said that small groups were the best kind. A few weeks before, when the group first started, I'd considered asking Alfred and Abner to come along, but then I decided I needed the time away from them to charge my spiritual batteries, without their constant drain. They could find their own group.

Phil and Mary were our hosts and leaders. Phil was a middle-aged insurance salesman; he'd done alright, too. He looked like Robert Duval on a good day. Their house was on the North Shore, and wife Mary was happy to live there, sitting as she was among the elite, who, she said, were in desperate need of salvation. Mary was keen on evangelism, and, according to her, the rich probably needed more saving than anyone else. That made sense. Mary was kind and sincere, and, when the subject of lost souls came up, her bright eyes flashed, sparked from a sharp inner desire to get the job done. Phil and Mary seemed to lack any serious marital issues, a loving couple who got along, an inspiration to us all.

And then there were middle-aged Esther and Bill. Esther was tall with straight blonde hair—not her natural color—a thin face and piercing eyes. Those eyes of hers alternated between expressing loving concern and something I was unable to get a handle on. Bill was short, stout and along for the ride. He owned a few of his own furniture stores. Thanks to Bill, Esther was well heeled, and she liked it that way.

Rounding out our group was George, a young man about my age. He reminded me of me in a way. He was good looking, had an average build, but unlike me, he was bordering on chunky, and his hair was sandy, not dark like mine, and it had no curl. He had no distinguishing marks. But he was a sad man, something to do with his wife. He hadn't opened up about it yet, but our hope was that he would. George was a carpenter, who did alright, but financially he was out of his league with the rest of us. I couldn't help wonder if I had chosen this group because we were all well off, except for George. All things considered, we were a good group, a typical soul-searching church group, studying the Prayer of Jabez, which was a perfect fit for us because we were all expecting to get even more blessings out of this life, except for George, who seemed to have his doubts.

Phil opened our meeting with a prayer, but he hesitated between thanking God for the day and a request his mind was too slow in formulating, which gave Esther an opening to override Phil with a prayer of her own. Her prayer was long, but not totally controlling. She ended by binding the wills of all her unsaved relatives, one by one, to the cross. Not one of them stood a chance. When she was done, we all felt better.

"Amen," Phil said.

"So," Mary said, "have we all had a good week?"

Nobody spoke.

"Well, then," Phil said, "how about an icebreaker?"

Our group tensed.

"If you were Elvis," Phil continued, spewing a laugh, "what kind of Elvis would you be?"

Mary said, "I would be the kind of Elvis who protected the rights of all those who don't have a voice."

Sensing there wasn't much more to add to that, George said, "I would be the kind of Elvis who never got married so I wouldn't have to go through all this pain...an' that."

Esther raised an eyebrow, and then laughed. "I hate this game," she said.

Her husband Bill said, "I never liked it, either."

Phil, sensing an icebreaker impasse, decided to move on. He said to his group, "Have you given any more thought to the proposed outreach idea we discussed last week?"

I decided to offer my suggestion. "How about giving out sandwiches and fruit drinks to the poor in the back alleys downtown?"

Mary offered me a broken smile. "That can be quite dangerous, you know, have you thought of that? And wouldn't we be much better served by ministering to the immediate neighborhood? You know what they say, "bloom where you're planted". We could give out food right here. For instance, we could volunteer to supply the oranges on Saturdays for the girls' spring grass hockey league."

"And that's a ton of oranges," husband Phil said, laughing.

Esther said, "Surely they must already budget for that."

"It's not the money, it's the gesture," Mary said. "We do all the cutting and delivering, too. It's a bother for them. I heard Mabel Greenstreet complaining about it the other day at the club. She said it was a silly tradition, which they could easily do without. What a bother, Mabel said. But I say, what about the girls? That's who we should be thinking of. So what do you think? It's also a chance for those hockey parents to see concerned, committed Christians in action."

While we tried to imagine serving God in this way, the sound of George choking back a sob grabbed our group's attention. Head down, he was tracing circles in the carpet with his left foot. "The way things are going," George said, "I'll probably never have any kids, let alone see them play field hockey, or anything else...an' that."

"Don't be silly," Esther said.

"Do you feel you have the freedom to share?" Phil said. "We've been noticing you haven't been yourself lately."

George prepared himself to share.

"Al's got another guy, I'm sure of it," George blurted.

"Al?" I said.

"Alabaster," Mary said, "George's wife."

So, Al's parents had been Flower Children, and by the sound of it, some of that free love had worn off on Al.

"I thought she was a Christian?" Bill said.

"Nominal," Mary said.

"Yes, nominal, too bad," Phil said.

I decided to do some digging.

"How do you know she's got another guy?" I said.

"She's out till all hours, and she's got some other job, besides her part-time job at Starbucks. She's studied acting, and now she's got a job doing that, or at least I think that's what she's doing. How am I supposed to know? She won't tell me anything about it. Says she has to keep it secret. What kind of job is that anyway, that you have to keep secret...an' that?"

"Have you ever wondered what those stars on the Starbucks logo represent?" Bill said.

"They've got Star in their name?" Mary offered.

"And the woman," Bill said, "a two-tailed Mermaid originally, quite obviously a figure for the Queen of Heaven, or Semiramis in Babylon, or Astarte in Egypt, or——"

Esther, interrupting husband Bill's hunt for corporate devils, said, "You don't mean pornography, do you, George?"

Shocked looks flew around the group and came to rest on George, who buried his head in his arms.

"Surely not," Mary said. "I've met Al, and she's just not that type."

"She's not a Christian," Phil said.

"She's nominal, though," Mary said.

"Certainly not a born-again, Spirit-filled believer," Bill said.

Reflecting, Mary said, "Do you think every Spirit-filled believer has to speak in tongues?"

"The gift's there to be used," Phil said, "you only have to exercise it."

Phil searched the room for agreement to his theological conclusion, but finding none he said, "Don't you worry, George, God can redeem her from that kind of lifestyle. Nothing's too hard for Him."

"Amen," Bill said.

George's face came out from hiding, and sobbing, he said, "She's not in that kind of lifestyle, that I know of. The problem is I don't have any proof either way."

Esther said, "You dabble in that line of work, don't you, Joe, it's sort of a hobby of yours?"

"I don't take divorce cases," I said.

George sobbed louder.

"Sorry, George," I said. "What I mean is, marriage is sacred, and ethically, as a Christian Detective, I don't take money for exposing adultery."

George's sob exploded.

"You could do it for free," Esther said. "Help a brother in the Lord out of his misery. Get some proof. Are you willing, Joe, but more importantly, are you able?"

I decided to set Esther straight on a few things, some important things, because I didn't like her tone and her questioning my status as a professional. There were some things you just didn't mess with, and a guy's profession was one of them. I was a detective, and a darn good one at that. And even though she was a sister in the faith, I had to take a stand, because if you didn't, the game was over. I knew I would always be challenged by those who would malign me and try to make me feel like less of a man, make me feel like dirt, just because I dared search the underbelly of the city for meaning to my existence. Somebody had to do it, so why not a Christian detective?

I engaged Esther's sharp, intimidating eyes and said, "I could probably help out."

"Do you hear that, George?" Phil said. "Joe's going to help you out."

George, now drained, said, "Do you think that would be right, I mean, to put a tail on Al…an' that?"

"Sure, if the tail's Joe," Bill said.

Esther winked at husband Bill. He'd said something right for a change.

"When you find out the truth," Mary said, "you will be able to put your mind to rest."

"It's settled then," Esther said. "Joe tails Al, gets the skinny on her, and then George will have gained the pertinent information on which to base his future life choices."

But George's face was blank now, his eyes staring over Esther's head at some distant movie, no doubt being projected by his fearful self.

"Will you do it, Joe?" George said.

"Sure, I can do it for a brother," I said, "as long as no money changes hands."

"Don't worry about that," George said.

"There, it's settled then," Esther said.

"Okay," Phil said, "let's move on…"

"What shall we do next?" Esther said.

"I was just about to…" leader Phil said.

"I know," Esther said. "Let's explore the Prayer of Jabez?"

"That's what I was just about say," Phil said.

"Good," Esther said. "Now last week we were talking about getting all our requests answered and being blessed and being kept from evil."

"Yes, evil," Bill said, "exactly what I've been trying to get at. Never mind Starbucks, have you ever looked closely at that all-seeing eye on the back of the American dollar bill? Are the Freemasons in charge or what—not to mention the Illuminati?"

Esther said, "Do you think those are appropriate topics for this homegroup, dear?"

Phil, deciding to defy Esther and reinforce his leadership, said, "Have you ever heard of chemtrails, Bill?"

"Sure," Bill said, "they're changing the weather with them. There's those ordinary vapor trails and then there's these chemtrails that hang up there a long time and do something to the atmosphere. It's the military or somebody doing it. They might even be poisoning us, who knows? We're all sicker than we used to be, if you haven't noticed."

"Now, Bill," Esther said, feigning patience, "you know there's no proof."

Uninterested in the group's conspiracy speculations, George whispered, "You will find out about Al, won't you, Joe…an' that?"

CHAPTER FOUR

"We're just gonna sit here for the rest of the day and into the night, ain't we?" Abner said. "I've had more fun than this scroungin' fer empties in an alley." Abner sprang up to look out the window, his dark blue eyes no doubt searching for the nearest alley.

"Let's not upset the boy," Alfred said, "he's got a lot of adjustments to make."

Alfred had that right. I had greater responsibility now. It was my duty to mentor Alfred and Abner in the faith, and at the same time run a private detective business. They were Baby Boomers. The Lord knew it wasn't going to be easy.

"The way yer goin'," Abner said, "there's still a good chance you'll end up livin' under cardboard in an alley."

I wondered when I should let Abner in on the fact that I was his spiritual leader, not to mention the fact that in this earthly realm he was working for me now. Maybe he thought I needed him more than he needed me. Who knew?

Alfred began thumbing through *Charisma* magazine, his chin elevated so he could see through the bottom lenses of his wire-framed bifocals.

"Did you know speaking in tongues is supposed to be part of your normal Christian experience?" Alfred said.

I recognized a teachable moment, and said, "No kidding."

"It says here you're supposed to be baptized in the Spirit, and then the evidence is, you start speaking in other languages."

"Well, I'm not positive that always happens," I said. "No I wouldn't count on it, not for sure, I mean."

Tongues? Why did Alfred have to find the most controversial subject he could find to dwell on? Mentoring was tough. Sure, we were going to a Charismatic Church now, but the congregation didn't speak in tongues much anyway; at least I hadn't heard any. Those Pentecostals started it. If they hadn't, there would be fewer divisions in the Church today. No, that was wrong; it was the disciples who started speaking in other languages on the Day of Pentecost. That's when the real trouble began. As for me, a dyed in the wool Charismatic, I wasn't sure if the Holy Spirit was advocating that sort of behavior these days or not.

"I'm already speaking in tongues," Alfred said.

"You are?" I said. "When did that start?"

"Almost from the beginning, when He healed me."

The best course of action was to pass the tongues issue on to Pastor Bernard to deal with. That was his job, pastoring the Church of the Manifest Presence, where anyone could join, no matter who you were, as long as you were repentant and remained faithful, although CMP did tend to attract a certain crowd, an upscale crowd of Charismatics, whatever that word signified these days, the word Charismatic kind of losing its meaning in the 21st century, what with postmodernism rearing the back of its ugly head. And why did Alfred have to get himself healed, too, causing more controversy. But I couldn't complain about that too loud, since I was the one who prayed for his healing, his clogged arteries zapped clean while he was sitting on his hospital bed waiting for the bypasses to be installed. God did the healing, of course, but without me saying the words, who knew what the outcome might have been? So why did Alfred feel it necessary to keep secrets from me, his mentor?

"Why didn't you tell me?" I said, sweeping the controversy under the rug for now. "How am I going to help you grow in the faith if you don't tell me when you've grown? And what if it's not healthy growth?"

Abner said, "Let's hear ya make some of them queer sounds."

"That's not how you do it, on demand," Alfred said. "And besides, it's mostly private."

"So ya think yer better than us now, I suppose you'll be castin' out demons next."

Alfred ignored Abner and resumed his reading. Alfred often surprised me. He seemed to have a growing relationship with God. How did that work, since he didn't ask me much? As for Abner, his cynicism remained intact, but to his credit, he had been staying sober. His many years of alcohol abuse were dragging on him, but for now, he was keeping the demon rum at bay.

"Why don't we just go fer lunch," Abner said, "or have we all started a fast?" Abner made a sour face, and continuing on a roll, said, "Yeah, if we have to fast, I've had a lot of experience in my time not eatin'. Course it was never my idea. I spent most of the last ten years tryin' to keep from fastin', but if I have to go without, I know how to do 'er. I remember once, I didn't eat solid food fer three weeks…at least I think it was that long. Hard to tell, hard to remember, the grape keepin' me alive."

"No, Abner, we're not fasting," I said.

No, we weren't fasting. I knew that for sure. Still, I wasn't hungry, for food at least. I was hungry to get our new case on track.

But what was I to do with Alfred and Abner? I'd been having my challenges with them ever since I opened up *Bell, Booker, and LaFlam*. The mentoring road ahead looked rough. Booker was an alias chosen by Alfred to keep the Spelunkers off his ex-hit-man trail. But until Sissy arrived on my penthouse doorstep, there was no sign the Spelunkers had been after us. I'd have expected that with our inside knowledge of their insidious scheme and Alfred's defection they would have sought revenge before now. It was strange, mighty strange. We could do them a lot of harm, even though we hadn't figured out a way yet, but they didn't know that, or did they? Or maybe they knew that Alfred got saved, and they thought we were harmless Christians now. But we couldn't afford to let our guard down. You never knew with these Spelunking, one-worlder types. They lurked underground, and who knew when they'd decide to put a couple of slugs into our redeemed hides? You couldn't slack off in my line of work at the best of times, but now we also had the burden of carrying the knowledge of the ages: *Spelunkers Global* was set to take over the world, and there wasn't a blessed thing the average Joe could do about it, because the fix was in. The governments of the world, the major corporations, the media giants, all were controlled by this underground menace. But who would believe us, three shamuses with an axe to grind, even if we did muster the guts to blow the whistle on those malignant players in the Spelunking scene? And who in authority could we trust to blow the whistle to, because who knew who-was-who in this game of world domination? That inside information wasn't listed anywhere, not even on the Internet. No, there was no hope to be found there.

So, what was I to do now? Not right now, sitting here; that wasn't the question I was trying to have answered; I could handle right now, but what was I to do for the rest of my life? I knew you were supposed to take it one day at a time, and if you strung enough one-at-a-times together, you would end up with a life. But would it have been a life that counted? Sure, your life would have counted in the sense that you did your time, but would it have meant anything? I knew my eternal meaning. I'd read the ending of the Book, and the ending pretty well took care of eternity. But what about my meaning on this planet? It was the here-and-now I had to get straight. What was the scope of my earthly mission? That was the question. I was a private detective with limitless potential. That was a fact. Another fact was that I needed exciting and intriguing cases to keep my sleuthing juices flowing. And I was sure Sissy's case would do just that; it was a case that had the potential to define my meaning here and to expand my world. Why? Because the Spelunkers were involved, that's why. Sure, I'd lost my moorings when my ship came in. Having all those greenbacks took a little getting used to. I was loaded now. Say what you wanted, my new mother was generous. She'd let me have enough do-ray-me to set me up in a dozen private eye offices, in a dozen penthouse apartments in a dozen towns. There was no price on guilt, leaving me like she did with her sister all those years, so she could marry rich and live rich and think rich, while I spent thirty odd years wondering who my father was, and thinking my first mother was my mother, who, as it turned out was really my aunt, and my dad who was dead in my mind showed up alive, the whole time not knowing I existed, because my real mother, who was now my second mother, hadn't told him either, so she could live the good life, rich and happy, in the American way.

"Sissy's a pawn," Alfred said, tossing his magazine onto the coffee table. "She's been sent to draw us in, particularly you." Alfred raised his eyebrows at me.

"I'm immune to that kind of thing now," I said in my defense.

I was hurt by Alfred's insinuation.

"Yer a real tree of righteousness, alright," Abner said.

"Let's not go there," Alfred said to Abner, "we don't want to get any further off track, since we wasted most of the morning already."

"You just went there," Abner said. "Why can't I?"

"So what have you got? Have you turned up anything new on the case," I said, to put an end to their bickering.

"Oh, listen to him," Abner said, "our mentor askin' us to do all his work."

"Who's mentoring who?" I said.

"What?" they said in unison.

"Okay, who's mentoring whom?"

They looked at each other. I had them there.

"Okay, Mr. Mentor," Abner said. "I've been lookin' at all this stuff about the Great Tribulation in this book I been readin'. There's pre-trib, and mid-trib, and post-trib. Do you mind explainin' some of that?"

"Abner, we're trying to focus on the case," Alfred said.

"Seems nobody's sure when this rapture thing happens," Abner continued. "I'm not so sure what the rapture is either. It's like flyin' up in the air or somethin'."

I decided to exercise my authority. "We can talk about that later," I said.

More ornery than usual, Abner said, "There's nothin' but trouble ahead. Ya can't trust nobody with yellow eyes, and she purrs to boot."

"We all know we can't trust her," Alfred said.

I said, "Well, maybe, but she's still..."

"See what we mean?" Alfred said.

"Ya, he's no tree of righteousness," Abner said to Alfred.

They were right. I was a sucker, and maybe celibacy was the best road for me.

"We could just wait to see what their next move might be," Alfred said.

"Great," Abner said, "more sittin' here, day and night."

"Or," Alfred said, "we could bait the hook."

"Don't look at me," Abner said.

Anticipating our next move, I said, "How?"

"I've got contacts. I could send out a few feelers."

"Wouldn't that be dangerous for you?" I said.

Alfred studied me and then shook his head at me in a way that might have been interpreted as disgust.

"Right," I said. "Well, what do you think, Abner?"

"Feel away, anything's better than sittin' here day after day, waitin' fer the Tribulation."

"Okay, if we're all agreed," Alfred said. "That's what I'll do. But this whole thing is fishy. I don't understand why they don't just kill us. It would be easy enough. It doesn't make sense."

I didn't want to bore Alfred with the fact that nobody ever died in my cases.

"Sense or no sense," I said, "there's such a thing as timing."

Alfred shook his head at me and then put his index finger to his chin, like he was posing for one of those pictures that try to make you look thoughtful and intelligent. How did they get people to pose like that? What stories did photographers invent to convince people to get their pictures taken with their fingers pointing at their own chins? God only knew.

Alfred said, "Okay, I'll make a call. But it still stinks. They should just kill us."

"I know why they don't," I said. "It's because nobody ever dies in my cases."

Alfred looked at Abner and then at me, and next he did something I'd never seen him do before. He began to giggle, like I'd said something funny. His giggling then exploded into a roaring fit. Abner and I watched him turn red.

Coming up for air, he said, "Has anybody ever suggested that you might be in denial?"

"Have you been talking to my Aunt Margaret?" I said.

CHAPTER FIVE

The trip to Seattle was smooth and uneventful. Alfred had offered the Spelunkers some bait that was hard to resist. His past experience as one of their hit-men had not been wasted. He knew the score. He knew what bait was. He knew what they'd fall for.

We were sitting in the dark, in the rain, outside Little Mama's Pizza joint on Fifth. It was 11:11 on the limo's clock. The Mercedes was a dream to wait in. I was behind the wheel, Alfred was riding shotgun, Abner lounged in the back. We were waiting for the rats to come out of the sewer, so to speak. Alfred had sent a message, code name Dano, through one of his old Spelunker channels, offering to exchange our silence for our lives. The deal was that we wouldn't blow the whistle on the whole diabolical bunch of them, as long as they didn't bump us off. A neat plan. I'd examine our scheme's ethics later. I knew from experience that an error in moral judgment reaped heavy consequences in this line of work. That was one of the challenges of being a Christian detective. Compromise and consequences. Well, in fact, it wasn't compromise; it was lying, lying for a purpose. And since our lie was just bait, that was okay. That wasn't lying, that is until I blew the whistle on them. And then the lie, or bait, would have been worth it. Lying to save the world from domination by low-lifes had to be an exception to the rule. It was a white lie really, like white witches. No, that wasn't right. White witches were just as much witches as black witches, but were white lies the same as black lies? Or were there black lies? I'd never heard anyone call them black lies before. For that matter, were they called black witches? And why was I getting so confused, so tangled up in my mind?

"If we're not sittin' at the office, we're sittin' somewhere else," Abner said. "Waitin', all we do is wait. If I'd known this was what private eyein' was all about, I'd of thought twice."

"It puts three square meals in front of you every day, doesn't it?"

"No need to get cruel," Abner said.

He was right. I was failing as a mentor. I was failing as a detective. I was failing in the mating game. I was a failure in my homegroup. I was failing as a human being. I was a failure, and not only a failure, but a failure also in denial and on the verge of major depression. I caught myself. There I was again feeding a negative attitude. I had to learn how to speak life into my life and into the lives of others, and to think life-giving thoughts, so that my mind would find liberation from the constant negative drone of the human condition and be immune to excessive thinking. But it was so hard.

"Sorry," I said.

Abner said, "Oh yeah, that's okay, I know. I had too many advantages when I was young. Didn't know how to handle 'er. Too much fer me. I never had yer advantage though. I grew up a heathen. My folks never knew the gospel."

"I said I was sorry."

"Who's that?" Alfred said.

"Where?" I said.

"Coming out of the alley beside Mama's," Alfred said.

Sure enough. The Dealmaker had arrived. He was clad in nifty hiking boots, sweatshirt, and Dockers, an umbrella hiding his face. He trotted over to my high-class Mercedes, leaning forward, like a bipedal uprooted toadstool, steeling itself against the wind-blown rain.

"He don't look dangerous," Abner said.

I powered the passenger window down, startling Alfred. The Dealmaker crouched and lifted his umbrella. He was in his forties, average build, short brown hair, no distinguishing marks, except for the scar descending from his left cheek down under his lower lip and then ascending again to halt just below his right cheek. His face was grim.

"Mind if I join you," he said, and shook his umbrella.

"Get in," Alfred said, thumbing at the back seat.

Abner slid over, mumbling, "Sit, that's all we do is sit."

The Dealmaker slammed the door of my Mercedes.

"Go easy," I said.

"Drive," he said.

"What do you mean, drive?" Alfred said.

"Yeah, who's in charge here?" I said.

"Ya might just want to do what he says," Abner said.

Then I saw it, in my rearview, the glint of a pick-axe, poised to strike, the kind of short-handled pick-axe you might find in the hand of your average Spelunker.

"You're not the only one packing heat," I said.

"Just drive," Alfred said.

I put my foot into it, and my silver sled accelerated away from the curb and into the dark, wet, monotonous night. Where were we going? That was the question. The Dealmaker had the upper-hand, and in it was a pick-axe ready to split Abner asunder. Maybe the deal was off. Maybe they were going to drop us dead in an alley, like three worthless slugs, the kind you spin into a pop machine and they drop straight through, not even genuine enough to spit you out a soda. I caught myself. I'd been whirling the negativity CD again in my mind. Thinking positive was hard. But where were we going?

"Where are we going?" Alfred said.

I saw the Dealmaker lower his axe.

"Kids," Abner mumbled. I admired his bravado, since that was all he could muster.

"You boys, don't you get nervous," the Dealmaker said. "We're all friendly, real friendly. You be friendly, too."

"Okay, so we're all friends," Alfred said. "Now where are we going?"

"To the Cave on Fourth Street."

"You mean the Night Club?" I said.

"You got it."

"Clever," I said. "Nobody would be looking for you there."

"Nobody knows enough to be looking for us anywhere, except for you, and you and you. And none of you will be telling anyone, will you?"

In my rearview, the Dealmaker's face doubled up with laughter.

"No we won't, Dealmaker," I said, "that's why we've set up this meet."

"And we want to make sure you won't, but we want to do it friendly like. We want us all to get along. One big happy family. We're not some kind of evil organization. See, I'm putting my pick away. No problem."

Not evil? Who was this guy? Who was he kidding? Spelunkers Global, planning to take over the planet, and they weren't evil. Dealmaker had a funny world view.

"Do you know a guy named Jake Dano, Dealmaker?" I said.

"Dano?"

"Yeah, about 6'7', with a Kung Fu moustache."

"Oh, yeah, Dano, he had a tough time. Wait, here we are, there's the parking lot, pull around back."

I wondered why the Dealmaker referred to Dano in the past tense. Maybe Sissy was worried for good reason.

"How do we know who and what you've got waiting for us in there?" Alfred said.

"We have to trust one another in this new world, in this new world of peace that's coming," Dealmaker said.

I parked and looked over at Alfred, and then I turned to Abner. Neither of them was happy. But we didn't have much choice. We were the ones who'd called the meeting.

"Okay, Dealmaker," I said, "let's do it."

We climbed out of my new Mercedes, whose skin shimmered in the low light of the silvery neon, and followed the Dealmaker into the Cave's back entrance.

"One other thing," he said, turning.

"Yeah?"

"Stop calling me Dealmaker. The name's Chuckles."

Once inside, we descended a spiral staircase, Chuckles in the lead. So where were we going? I knew we were going down, but were we going down to the end, or was this just the beginning? And why had I been entrusted with saving the world? There was no logical answer, but I wouldn't let anyone down, although no one in the world really knew yet they could be let down by me, and if they had known, they probably wouldn't have entrusted me with the future of the world. Some things were just hard to figure.

"At least for a change we're not sittin'," Abner said, huffing and puffing, as we continued our journey downward into the bowels of the Cave.

We came to a landing and then made a sharp right through a doorway and into a large room, about the size of my penthouse office. But this room was cavern shaped, and unlike my office, which exuded high-class, this cavern's decor was black paper maché, no doubt a favored medium of the Spelunkers' interior decorator. The fake candles, nestled in the maché outcroppings on the walls, emitted a green light. A colony of fake bats hung insolently from the ceiling. In one corner, two black figures sitting at a table stirred at our approach.

"Here they are," Chuckles said.

A creepy voice crept out of the inky darkness, a voice that might have oozed from a snake whose hiss had been tamed, since the voice also had a charming, soothing edge to it.

The voice said, "We're going to do it, you know. You should know, shouldn't you Alfred? Your name is Alfred, isn't it? You're in the center of it now. We're ready to do it. If they don't know, at least you should know, Alfred. We're going to do it, aren't we?"

"Reminds me of that time," Abner said, "back in '92, I think it was, when I had the DTs in that alley in Tucson. Pitch black and things talkin' at me. Was only in the detox a week that time though, the nurses there..."

"Abner," Alfred said, "we can hear about your sordid exploits some other time."

And then I heard it, a familiar wheeze, from the other figure at the table. I knew it must have been coming from the throat of someone I'd met before. Figure two had to be Sissy. But who was figure one? The table and chairs glided forward into the candle-light, a nifty trick. Then the two figures rose out of the shadows to greet us. Figure one with the slick tongue looked to be about 400 pounds. He was bald and wore a black tuxedo. Figure two had blonde hair. Sissy Smith had black hair, but this one, figure two, with the blonde hair, looked exactly like Sissy. The nose was a dead giveaway, not to mention the yellow eyes. The hair looked natural, but had to be a wig.

"Is that you, Sissy?" I said.

"She sure don't look like no Sissy," Abner said.

A petulant figure two said, "No, I'm not Sissy. Can't you tell? I'm so sick of it. It doesn't matter what you do, it's always the same."

Full-figured one said, "Shut it, Crusty."

His sweet, hypnotic voice was now harsh. I made a mental note of his mood swing.

"Twins," he said to us, by way of explanation, "but they're not alike at all."

Ah, so Sissy and Crusty were twins.

"You've met my sister, then?" Crusty said.

"Yeah," I said, "she hired our firm to do some work for her."

"What kind of work?" Crusty said.

"To find someone."

"Jake, it was Jake Dano, wasn't it? Crusty said. "Well, she can't have him back." She then turned to the portly snake and added, "She can't, can she, Papa?"

The head on top of the rotund tuxedo nodded forward, reflecting green in the wall-candles' light, and then it reared back and spewed a spontaneous laugh at the hanging fake ceiling-bats. Recovering from his outburst, Papa said to Crusty, no doubt to soothe her, "Sissy is simply confused right now."

"What 'er we here for again?" Abner said.

Papa's face soured, sputtered, and then wheezed. Crusty followed her Papa's lead.

"It must run in the family," Abner said. "You can't be livin' underground without some consequences."

Sure, Crusty was a little sick, and sure she was spoiled, you could see that, but there was something about her that grabbed me. And you could see that she'd had it tough, the way life could be tough when you were born a twin underground. Sure, it was the elite underground, but what difference did that make? It was still the underground. Riches hadn't done me much good so far either. Sure, I didn't have to worry about money anymore, but now there were other things to worry about, things I wouldn't have considered before, like wondering how I would know if a woman was attracted to the real me or whether she just wanted my money? It wouldn't be that way with Sissy—or with Crusty for that matter. We were equals on about the same rung of the social ladder. So anything was possible. Spelunkers Global, when I was through with them, would be no more, and Sissy and Crusty, well, they would be redeemed. That would be my goal, and just to keep myself honest, I would commit to celibacy. That would keep my motives straight and pure. And there was probably a cure for their respiratory conditions too, once they were liberated from their dank lives.

"Here's the deal," the wheezing caveman said. "We're really a friendly bunch. You will understand that soon. Chuckles, bring them something to sit on."

Chuckles slid us over three paper maché boulders. We perched on them and listened to the portly Spelunker sing the "we all just want to get along" tune. He told us there were opportunities to be had in the New World Order. All we had to do was see it their way. It was a pitch for compromise and part of their whole seduction package. There would be temptations, ways to lure even the strongest into the demonic realm of the anti-Christ system. Fascinating. I was all ears.

I watched Crusty, while her corpulent Papa spun his web. You could tell she loved her Papa. You could see there was love there, even though they were on an evil course. How did that work? I guess there was always hope. I stifled my sappy thoughts and returned my mind to the business at hand.

Finishing his spiel, Papa folded his arms and laid them on his protruding mid-section expanse.

"So, you see, we need men like you," he concluded.

"But what do we have to do to stay alive?" Abner said.

"Have you not been listening?" Alfred said.

The tuxedo grunted and raised himself to his feet. He looked like a bald, gluttonous nun with a bad habit. Lithe Crusty sidled to his side.

"Of course, we want to give you time to think about it," Papa said. "We want you to realize that we are friendly. We aren't pushy. You will see that we are all one big happy family here, and we are positive that once you get to know us you will see the light."

Crusty said, "And when you see Sissy again, don't believe a word she says."

"And you, Joe," her Papa said, "we've had an eye on you, and we see the potential. At first, we just wanted to eliminate you, didn't we Alfred? But since you seemed so hard to get rid of, we wondered why, and then we did some research. A few things have come to light since that initial unfortunate misunderstanding. There's been considerable speculation, surrounding your birth date and the alignment of the stars at that time, and your ancestry. We think you might be one of us, one of the Twelve, who will serve directly under Thirteen. There are only five of us now, and you just might be number Six."

It was the old come on. I wasn't born yesterday, as they seemed to know. Joe LaFlam wasn't going to be conned by the oldest trick in the book, the enticement of power. Power, who needed it? I had enough trouble as it was. People thought power brought security, but I knew from my thirty odd years on the planet that it only brought fame, success, and people bowing down to you. Well, I didn't need it. My work was enough, and I had the almighty bucks to back me up now, too, even though the dollar wasn't all that mighty these days. Even so, I had enough dough. I was secure enough in my wealth not to fall for the old power temptation.

And then he said it. It wasn't spelled out, but he said it.

"Oh, by the way, Joe, you know your family's business?"

"Huh?"

"Things can change," Papa said, "if this doesn't go our way."

"I can't wait to hear your answer, Joe," Crusty said.

"And don't worry about how to get in touch with us," Papa said. "We will contact you."

Papa nodded at Chuckles, who, obeying his boss's cue, escorted us out of the room. I took one last look at Crusty over my shoulder and wondered what I would be without my new family's money. And then I remembered. I would still be me.

CHAPTER SIX

Back at the office we sat. We were glum, and it was late. The sound of silence rang in my ears, magnifying the background rapping of the pelting rain, the heavy intermittent drops slapping the windows. Alfred got up and started to throw darts at my executive dartboard.

"Could lose it all," I said.

"They could do it in an instant," Alfred said, his dart finding the triple six.

"It don't bother me," Abner said. "When you ain't got nothin', you got nothin' to lose."

"Couldn't you at least try to encourage the boy?" Alfred said.

"Didn't ya just say he could lose it in an instant?" Abner said. "Have ya got different rules for me and you or somethin'?"

Abner looked at me for recognition. He'd won one. Alfred hit the double twenty with his last dart and then sat down.

"Who is Thirteen?" I said to Alfred.

"I heard about those witches' covens," Abner said. "They spend their time castin' spells and sacrificin' stuff."

"It's not a coven," Alfred said. "I don't know all the details. They didn't tell us hired hands much about what would happen afterward, when they surfaced. But I know this much. They're going to divide the world into twelve jurisdictions, each ruled by one of the elite, and Thirteen, alias Lord Maitraya, will rule them all. And that's pretty well all I know about it."

So, their plan was to have twelve jurisdictions ruling over the whole world. The fix was in. But at least I had a new case-name to file, under T for Twelve, The Case of, the case to end all cases. The other choice was under T for Thirteen, The Case of, sort of a baker's dozen Case of Twelve. But that was no good. The world was being divided into Twelve not Thirteen, and Twelve was an even number, and Thirteen was unlucky, though, of course, I didn't believe in luck. Either way, I'd file it under T.

"Ya gonna do it?" Abner said.

"Do what?"

"Ya got a darn good offer to join up and rule part of the world. Ya don't get that kinda offer every day. And I think that Crusty girl with the breathin' problem took a likin' to ya. That Dano don't stand a chance."

Alfred said, "What are you talking about, Abner?"

"Ah, don't look so serious, I was just testin' him."

"Try to stop it," Alfred said.

"Sure," Abner said, "I was only seein' if it was worth stickin' around, and whether he's gonna be off rulin' the world and leavin' us here to fend for ourselves."

Alfred gave him a final warning contained in a stare.

"Okay, I'll stop. But I got an idea; let's just sit here for the rest of the night."

Alfred pretended to ignore him.

"Maybe you should get some sleep," I said.

"I'm outta here," Abner said.

"Fine," Alfred said. "Let's go."

"Yeah," I said, "that long trip south of the border and back can take a lot out of you."

Alfred looked at Abner. "South of the border?" they said.

"Oh, right, never mind," I said. "Go ahead, I'm going to sit here for a while."

"Figures," Abner said.

Alfred and Abner left me to sort out the evening. I had a lot to sort out. It wasn't every day you got an offer to rule the world, and then if you didn't play along, you would lose your family's fortune. It was a no-win situation. On the one hand, a pact with the devil and a life of evil ease, on the other, a one-way trip to the alley of destitution, only then I'd have the rest of the family sharing my cardboard. The weight of responsibility was heavy to bear. But I knew there was a way out, the only way out. Straight ahead. The only way out was through. I had to bust the whole bunch of them, especially Thirteen. But then what about Sissy and Crusty? What was my responsibility to them, especially Sissy? I'd taken her case, after all. I'd given my word, the word of a Christian detective, and if you couldn't trust the word of a Christian detective, whose word could you trust in this crazy, mixed-up, chaotic world, where you tried to stay out of trouble and torment but they followed you around anyway, like those rogue patches of ugly hair that grew on your shoulder blades?

I needed to see Sissy again. And I needed a plan, a deliberate direction that would lead me in measured steps to Thirteen. I knew the most obvious track to follow; it was playing a tune in the back of my mind. I knew there was no sense playing it for Alfred and Abner. They wouldn't want to hear it. Instead, they would insist on singing their favorite we-know-better song. Alfred had probably already guessed my tune, and Abner most likely had, too. But there was no other way. There was no question about it now. I knew it had to be. It was fate, though I didn't believe in it. I had to go undercover. I had to become one of them. To save the family and the world, I had to become a Spelunker. And not just any Spelunker, but one of the Twelve, number Six likely. I would tell Papa I was ready to be groomed to be one of the elite. And I would tell Sissy I would find her Jake, which would fulfill my detective's responsibility. And since I was joining the side of evil, my family's fortune would remain safe. I gulped at the thought of my first real undercover mission. I knew I would need to learn the sure-footed steps of a tightrope walker, as I danced my way between the devil and poverty, between destruction and freedom, and, of course, between staying on the rope and falling off to my death below.

CHAPTER SEVEN

The next morning I decided to skip going straight to the office. I'd
let Alfred and Abner open up the store. My morning mission was to
check out Al and see what the score was with her acting career. Poor
George. I felt for the guy. He needed all the help I could give him.
But for the grace of God, I went. What if I had married and the wife
had strayed from the straight and narrow? How would I have felt?
There was no real way of knowing for sure, but I did know one
thing, it wouldn't feel good. And I knew another thing for sure,
when your brother was in need you reached out a hand to help,
which in this case was putting a tail on his missus. I didn't need
Alfred and Abner for this one. I was driving solo this morning in
my Mercedes. I would show up at the office in my own good time.
My hours were my business. They weren't running the show. Still,
it would be common courtesy to let them know I had a new case.
No, on second thought, I would just let them know I wouldn't be
in. I put on the headset.

"Pen?" I said.

"Oh, it's you."

"Put me through to Alfred and Abner."

"Put you through?"

"Okay, put me through, please."

"Certainly."

She buzzed and they answered.

"Alfred?" I said.

"Oh, it's our mentor," Abner said.

"I'm not coming in this morning," I said.

"Shouldn't we be working on Sissy's case?" Alfred said.

"You guys go ahead, and I'll catch up with you this afternoon."

"Congratulations," Abner said, "for once you're not going to just sit here all day."

"What's up?" Alfred said.

"Can't tell you now. You know, it's just personal."

"Stay out of trouble," Alfred said.

"Ya, and we'll just sit here waitin' fer ya," Abner said.

"Fine."

I beeped them off. I was an adult, and I could handle a case by myself, the way I did before I hired them. I reminded myself that I was the one doing them a favor; I was the one who gave them a job. Then I forgave myself for being so petty.

That done, I pointed my Mercedes toward the Starbucks at 41st and Main, where Al poured her lattés and no doubt plotted her rise to stardom, hardened to the fact her ascent began in the pit of human depravity. But maybe I was judging her too soon. After all, I only had George's suspicions to go on, and I knew from my experience—from what I'd seen on TV mostly—that a husband's ability to see the facts was often blinded by stupidity. I resolved never to be that way myself, if I was ever given the chance, and if celibacy wasn't my calling.

I parked my luxurious sled outside Starbucks and wondered about the wisdom of going in. My thirst won out. What was the harm? I headed for the door. Outside, seated at tables under umbrellas, smokers sucked their lives away, sipping their bitter brew. I tried not to judge. Once inside, I joined the queue, my fedora low over my eyes, though she wouldn't have known me from Adam, even if she did get a good look at me. There were three of them working behind the counter, all women. I picked her out though, from George's description. She was a little on the tall side, not too thin, her hair brown, the kind of brown you got used to, day after day, the same person, every morning and every night, leading a brown mundane life, serving the coffee, George hammering nails, all for what? Every shot of the nail gun, driving home his despair, every cut of the saw, a reminder of the threat of separation. Yes, I could see why she might take a chance, why she might step out in a way that she thought would bring relief from the ordinary, the plodding day-to-day reality of never-ending sameness, not unlike the gut-wrenching toil of penguins procreating at the Pole. I snapped out of it. I had to stay positive. Life was too tough otherwise. My detective's insight concluded that Al and pornography weren't a match made in heaven. Still, with some makeup. Her face was plain, but nice. But no, she wasn't the type at all. George's imagination had to have taken him for a ride. My turn was up, and I ordered a Caramel Frappuccino from Al.

"Size?" she said.

There was a good chance her voice might have made it in the movies, but did she have the talent? That was the question. Voices were a dime a dozen in the movie scene's heartless torso.

"Venti."

Al raised an eyebrow. A mid-morning Frappuccino wasn't a sin. And besides, it was closer to noon. I paid and waited, sizing up the room. I thought I saw Al shoot me a glance, like she was giving me the quick once over. But I wasn't sure. One of her caffeine comrades buzzed the sweet juice together and set the result on the counter. I nodded, grabbed the heavy mix, and looked for a place to suck it down. The tables were full, so I exited and headed for my Mercedes. A stray mutt gave my Frappuccino the eye, but I held it close and then climbed into my leather haven. Inside and comfy, I took a drag on the straw, loving the moment, and then turned on the sound system to catch Peter, Paul and Mary singing "Puff the Magic Dragon"; the song had never sounded too Biblical to me. Comfy now, I waited for Al to exit at noon, when, according to George, her shift ended.

At 12:10, she hurried out the door and caught the Main Street bus for downtown. Bloated, the sweet delicate taste still lingering in the back of my throat, I wondered how many stops the bus would make before Al reached her destination. A Mercedes tailing a bus, how surreal my life was at times. I hung back the best I could, a few of the motoring public behind me, finding the time to lean on their horns. There was nothing I could do but follow slowly and wait for Al to make her move. To impress my fellow travelers, I put on my headset and faked talking on the phone, my eyes gazing off at the horizon, absorbed in the seriousness of my bogus conversation. They would never suspect I was tailing a bus to get the goods on my homegroup brother's wife, who was suspected of taking a not-so-lovely route to stardom. They would see me as an important man, in my Mercedes, talking on the phone, probably closing a major business deal? No dice. They were unimpressed. Their horns continued to sound. It was clear they didn't care about me or my life's challenges.

At Main and Hastings, she sprang from the bus and then walked north like a woman late for her hairdresser. Seconds later, she disappeared into a doorway. I made a covert pass and read the storefront sign: *Curly's Cuts*. I had some time to kill. I pulled into a taxi stand and waited. There was no reason to call Alfred and Abner; I didn't have to check in to tell them I would be delayed. I was the boss. Still, there was nothing else to do.

"Pen?"

"I'm here."

"Put me through...oh, thanks...Alfred?...Abner?...Alfred?... Abner?"

"They're not here," Pen said.

"Then why did you put me through?"

"That's what you were going to ask me to do, wasn't it?"

"Yes, but..."

"They'll be back at three, that's what they said to tell you when you called."

"Thanks, Pen, for your efficiency," I said.

We beeped each other off. So they were out for an extended lunch. But I didn't blame them. They had their lives to live. My thoughts about my partners were rattled by a hard rap on my window. I powered it down.

"Couldn't you hear me honking, this is a taxi stand, move this heap out of here."

"I'm sorry," I said, "I've driven hack before and I know the challenges you face."

"Just get out of here," he said.

I powered up my window and pulled out into the traffic. More horns. I would have to go around the block. As fate would have it—though, as a Christian, I didn't believe in fate—they were digging up the street. I made it around in about twenty minutes and then pulled again into the now vacated taxi stand. In my rearview mirror, I saw another taxi honking its way toward me. But, just in time, there she was, Al coming out, her hair brown and shoulder length, looking about the same. Oh, well. I pulled out, and away she went. About a block later, she ducked into another building. I drove on past and read the sign. Sure enough, my worst fears were realized. It was the location of Weirdest Name Possible Productions. So it was true. Al had sunk to the depths in a misdirected attempt to rise to the heights. But then again maybe she needed to take a downward journey to the bottom in order to get saved. Some people had to get to the end of themselves before they were able to come to the truth. But that reasoning wouldn't sit well with George. And I reminded myself that there was always hope. Just because it looked bad, didn't mean it was bad. I didn't have any proof that Al was on that old slippery slope of compromise. Maybe Weirdest Name Possible Productions was benign, and the name only sounded bad; maybe they were making clean corporate videos, or documentaries, or animated shorts, and she was only doing voices. Sure, she had a good voice. I'd do some digging and get the dope on WNPP, and then I'd know for certain. I liked Al, and I hardly knew her. I hoped for the best. Who wouldn't? She was a swell gal, Al was, and George was an okay guy. They made a great couple, and I was here to make sure they stayed that way. But there was no sense doing any more snooping now. I would get the goods on WNPP first, and then, if I had to crash their party, I would know what costume to wear.

CHAPTER EIGHT

The next morning I was playing along with Alfred and Abner and keeping my decision to go underground to myself.

"We can't keep stalling," Alfred said. "They're up to something, and we might as well find out what it is."

"Papa told us they would contact us," I said.

"They gave us an ultimatum," Alfred said. "We need to act before we run out of time."

"Let's not worry about it," Abner said. "Let's just sit here, day after day, waitin'. That's just our mentor's style."

Abner's discontent faded into the background, as the sun's rays, shafting through my penthouse windows, exposed the dust flecks flickering in the mid-morning light, the rain stopped for now, life in the city down below hanging onto the promise of spring's new birth. Then I remembered the strings. That's what the dust reminded me of, strings. Everything was created from strings. I saw it on Nova.

To underscore his boredom, Abner threw my fedora on the floor about ten feet away from his chair and began to flick playing cards at it.

According to Nova, everything was made of these tiny strings that vibrated. In effect, though the scientists wouldn't agree, the whole universe was humming along to God's tune. Nova said string theory united two other theories that were impossible to unite before. One theory explained everything big, and the other explained everything small. But the scientists had never been able to fit the two theories together until this whole string thing came along. But there was a problem. String theory was impossible to prove, because the strings were too small for anyone ever to see. If you were standing on Jupiter, for instance, and looking back at Earth with your naked eye a string would be the size of a mealy worm lunching on a carcass. We'd never be able to see one. So, science and all of us citizens here on earth were stuck for proof, which helped me to put our case in perspective. All I had to do was find Dano among the Spelunker underground, which seemed simple in comparison.

"You never did tell me how you and my Aunt Margaret met," I said to them both.

"And we're not likely to," Alfred said.

"Yer nosy questions are just yer way of stallin'," Abner said.

"I need to go out," I said. "I've got some private business I need to take care of."

"Keepin' secrets, are we?" Abner said.

"Seems to me like there are a few secrets being kept around here lately," I said, and winked.

"Touché," Abner said.

The ride downtown was sweet. I'd made a decision, and Alfred and Abner had responded like I was the boss of the team. Alfred didn't even try to take over. I was maturing. I felt that I was back on top of my game and in perfect form to help my homegroup brother George and at the same time strike a blow for all my brothers who had been cheated on by desperate wives gone wild. I would strike a blow for them all. As for my mother…sure, she'd dumped me for a rich guy, but who was I to judge? She'd come out of it okay, with all the dough, having shucked the dead husband, and now she was married to my real father. If she hadn't gone that route, she might have had to bring me up penniless and destitute, and who knows, by now, I might have ended up pickled in alcohol and frozen to death under cardboard, in some alley, in some city, in the Pacific Northwest.

I pulled into the parking lot across the street from the building that housed Weirdest Name Possible Productions. I had to find out if their studio was actually in there. I'd checked my sources, mostly the Internet, and if there was anything to know about WNPP, you sure couldn't find it. Whatever they were up to, their tracks were covered like a snowboarder outrunning an avalanche. As for me, the only way to go was through, and I intended to take that direct route for the sake of my homegroup brother George.

The door looked innocent enough. Weirdest Name Possible Productions was stenciled in block caps on the glass. Inside, a foxy, redheaded lady in her mid-thirties, her glasses hanging from silver strings, thrust her pointed face toward me and asked me my business.

"I heard you make movies here," I said.

"Do you have an appointment?"

"To see who?" I said.

"You would have to know that," she said.

I was getting nowhere fast. I needed a way in, so I decided to get to the point.

"A friend of mine, Al, told me about you."

"I don't know any Al. Are you sure you have the right address?"

"Her real name's Alabaster," I said.

"Hippie parents?" she said.

I nodded.

"No, we don't know any Alabaster, either."

"Have you got a client list?" I said.

"We don't give out confidential information, as I'm sure you must already know. Are you a private detective?"

I was flattered that she'd noticed.

"Bingo," I said. "I've got a dame I'm tracking who's on a slippery slide to hell. If I can catch up to her and slow her descent it will make my client a happy man."

"I get it, you're looking for work," she said.

"What kind of work have you got for me?" I said, playing along.

"I enjoy what you do, but we only take referrals."

I continued to go nowhere fast. This was no dumb redhead I was dealing with. There was more to her. She was one of those non-Christians you could end up loving more than your brothers and sisters in the faith. The ideal solution was to convert her, but then she would be even more difficult to get along with, since her reality would have changed. She would then be at odds with the world like the rest of us believers. It was easy to get along with the world when you were one of them, but if you stepped out of line, if you stepped into the Kingdom of God, all bets were off as far as the world was concerned. You were an outcast then. Your name was Christian.

"What are you staring at?" she said.

"Love your hair," I said.

"It's time for you to leave," she said, not unkindly.

"It's too bad, sweetheart; we could have made beautiful music together."

"No more auditions," she said. "We're not looking for your type."

"What type are you looking for?" I said.

"I'll have to call security if you don't leave."

"Don't get your shirt in a knot, sister; I know when I'm not wanted."

"I doubt that."

I turned tail and left the office. She was a sweet kid. I was glad I'd met her. She'd given me some hope, too. I doubted that a sharp cookie like her would be involved in such a sordid trade as the one George suspected his wife Al was into. Pornography was a plague on our planet, all caused by a pleasure center in the brain, programmed for procreation—I'd seen that on PBS, too—but its purpose was twisted by the corrupt vermin who prayed on the sons of men. Well, Al and George weren't going down that road if I could help it, their marriage destroyed, victims of the corruption and greed of others. No, not if Joe LaFlam had anything to say about it. But what was I going to do next? I needed another strategy. Head on hadn't worked. My only hope was to put the tail on Al again and see what I could turn up. I hoped the truth didn't turn out to be naked.

CHAPTER NINE

I was stalled again about my decision to go underground, so it was just as well I hadn't heard from Papa yet. On the other hand, Alfred and Abner were ready to confront the Spelunkers head on. I continued to keep secret my vow to go undercover, the one I'd made to myself, although I'd pretty well reached a conclusion about the scriptural question of whether vows made to oneself were binding. The scriptural answer was that even when they were made to God and not to oneself they were still Old Testament. That meant I was free to do what I wanted, vow or no vow. And, right now, I needed some breathing space. The excuse I gave Abner and Alfred for my stalling was that the spiritual principle of timing might be the key to our success, so there was no need to rush. The real reason for my delay was fear. It was easy to talk a good game, but when the threat of death stared you in the kisser, even if it wasn't allowed in my cases, the sweat dripping had a habit of stinging your eyes and clouding your view, so that you lacked the confidence to make a move.

I wasn't making much progress in George and Al's case, either. I almost didn't want to know. In fact, I didn't want to know. That's why I didn't take divorce cases, that and respecting the sanctity of marriage. Some said there was an adultery loophole in scripture. But that wasn't my business. I wasn't a theologian, I was a private detective, and a darn good one at that, and I wasn't going to fall for the temptation of taking divorce cases just to pocket some ill-gotten gain. In this case, though, George was a brother, and a homegroup brother, too, and I was doing it for free. Still, I wasn't getting any-where in the case. It felt like I was running on the spot in lead overshoes.

Church Sunday had been the regular fare. Nothing unusual came from the pulpit, and the after-service donuts and gab were uninspiring. I was beginning to lose interest in my new church. Sure, the home-group had potential, but who were these people in the Church of the Manifest Presence? Who were these church mates of mine? Sure, I lacked savvy in a few areas of life, or maybe in more than a few areas, but after thirty years of church, I knew the church score. I knew what made church tick. And, these days, she was ticking to new tunes. There were post-modern tunes, third-day tunes, emergent-church tunes, virtual church tunes, church in the marketplace tunes, and we-will-all-all-get-there-one-day tunes. My only consolation was the solid fact that God knew what he was doing. He probably had a plan that He alone knew, one we had already read in His Book but didn't understand, a plan different from the ones we had created for ourselves.

It was homegroup night again, and I was wrestling with whether or not I would have dinner at home. I found Aunt Margaret resting on the sofa. She had company coming, and I knew she preferred to entertain them alone.

"Are you going to your homegroup, dear?" Aunt Margaret said. "If so, are you going to tell me if you're having dinner with us?"

"When you were young, Aunt Margaret," I said, joining her on the sofa, "what church did you go to?"

"Oh, how I love it when you call me Aunt Margaret."

"Baptist?" I said.

"Oh, I didn't go to church, dear. Church wasn't popular with my generation. We much preferred doing our own thing."

"Then how did we end up going to the Baptist Church?"

"That happened after it all went…oh, never mind, dear, it's not worth going into. But we've now left the Baptists, haven't we, dear."

"I needed to move on," I said.

"Yes, I suppose the girls are nicer to look at in your new church, and there are certainly more of them. I wasn't all that thrilled about leaving the Baptists either, but since you decided to leave, I thought we should stick together, didn't I? Your new church doesn't really appeal to me, does it? I've told you often enough. I guess I'm still a Baptist at heart. And if it wasn't for Reverend Schuller on TV Sunday mornings, I don't know what I would do, though I much prefer the older man to the son..."

"I'm eating out," I said.

"You suit yourself, dear. I've got company coming, anyway."

Sure, she had company coming, and I hoped the whole thing wouldn't blow up in my face.

"It's none of my business, but don't you think you should choose between them?"

"I don't think you should judge, dear. Especially since your generation made that *Friends* show so popular."

"I hope it doesn't blow up in my face," I said. "I don't want to have to pick up the pieces."

"Don't be so melodramatic, dear. We're quite able to manage our own affairs."

Aunt Margaret was staring at the far wall, at the old picture hanging there of her and her friends in their hippie outfits, young and innocent and full of flower power; then, her wistful gaze intensifying, she added, "But it's not like that anymore. No, it never can be again."

Before she slipped over the edge, I said, "You're right, you know how to run your life, and I shouldn't try to interfere."

"Yes, that's true, dear," she said, exiting her '60s trance, "and isn't that the doorbell?"

"Yes, what else would it be?" I said.

"Carry on, dear. And don't worry about me."

Aunt Margaret rushed to the front door, slowing to straighten her flower sack before she ushered them in. There they were, dressed up for the evening, smiling their way through the door. I had to leave.

"Goin' out?" Abner said.

"Yes," I said.

"You can't stay?" Alfred said.

"He's got homegroup," Aunt Margaret said, "and who knows what else."

"McDonald's probably," Alfred said.

"Dear me," Aunt Margaret said, "have you seen that movie *Supersize Me*, where the man nearly dies?"

"His liver started to pack it up, just like he had cirrhosis," Alfred said.

"Oh, leave him alone," Abner said, defending me for a change, no doubt because of his sensitivity to the subject of cirrhosis.

"Have a fun time," I said, and left them there to sort out their evening.

CHAPTER TEN

I felt uneasy at the start of homegroup, because my digging into Al's production company hadn't turned up much yet, and I wasn't sure how to avoid George. He already knew his missus might be into something a little on the shady side after I'd phoned and told him I tailed her to WNPP. He'd already suspected the worst, so my news confirming his suspicions hadn't cheered him up. But I did offer him the hope that the company might still be on the up-and-up, and that maybe she was keeping her acting job secret so she could surprise him with some great role or other. He said he didn't need any of those kinds of surprises. So tonight I was sitting on pins and needles, hoping he wouldn't ask me what I'd found out about the company. Over a donut and Coke, he popped the question, like he really didn't want to know, and, as it turned out, I didn't know, which made him feel better. Then I told him I'd have something for him later in the week, and that seemed to satisfy him.

Our group was intact, Phil and Mary at the helm, Esther and Bill eager to begin, and George and I unsettled but willing. The plan was to continue our study of The Prayer of Jabez. Jabez seemed useful, and although I had all the money I wanted, I still needed, celibacy aside, a wife and some kids and a successful detective's career. The Prayer of Jabez, as we all knew, was a big prayer. It was deep, real deep, and popular. Its message had gone around the globe. And we all knew that mass marketing and promotion were good things when they were used to spread truth far and wide.

"We'll skip the icebreaker this week," Phil said.

"After all," Mary said, "we all know each other well enough now not to be so shy."

I knew they wanted us to open up, so we could have our hearts healed, but what was there to get at?

"What are we trying to get at?" I said.

"Community," Esther said. "We need to break down the walls between us. We are going to be spending eternity together, as one big happy family, and we might as well start now, learning how we fit together."

"You know what she means," Bill said. "Some of us are elbows, some of us are hands, some of us are less seemly parts."

"That's fine, thanks, dear," Esther said. "I think everyone gets the idea. So, George, anything further on Al?"

Phil and Mary exchanged glances, which let slip their anxiety about Esther once more taking control of the meeting.

"Joe's been a big help," George said. "He followed her down to some studio near skid row...an' that."

"But I don't know for sure yet what kind of movies they're making," I said.

"Well that's a big help," Esther said.

"Okay then, let's move on," Phil said.

"So what's the next step, Joe?" Esther said.

"I'm going to do some digging into who owns the company and find out what they've done in the past."

"...an' that," George added.

"Okay then," Phil said, "let's get into our book study for the evening."

"And what about you, Joe?" Esther said, ignoring Phil.

"What about me?" I said.

"What's your motivation? I mean, what's this private detective obsession all about?"

I could see Esther wasn't the pastoral type. She seemed to have a burr under her blanket, and I doubted there was enough itch cream in the world to cool her torment. Phil and Mary were the pastoral type, but Esther, bless her heart, was more forceful. She was driven to get the job done. I decided to play along. I didn't want to make a scene.

"Maybe some father issues, I don't know," I said.

"She isn't really making porn movies, is she?" George said to the chandelier.

"Let's try to stay on topic," Esther said to George.

Trying to retake charge of the meeting, Phil said, "If I heard you right, Joe, you seem to be relating your father issues to your choice of profession?"

"You can't get much more Freudian than that," Esther said. "He's really been looking for his dad, not lost kittens."

"But we don't believe in Freud," Bill said, "do we, honey?"

Esther froze husband Bill with a shot from the corner of her left eye.

"The Father heart of God," Mary said, "we all need more of the Father's Heart."

"Don't forget the Mother heart of God," Esther said.

"She's probably only doing commercials," George said.

"We certainly don't agree with calling God, Mother," Phil said.

"Neither do we," Bill offered.

"That's not the point," Esther said.

"But why won't she tell me?" George said.

"It's simple," I said, attempting to turn the discussion back to me. "I like what I do. I'm called to be a private detective, and it's my way of serving."

"Can you find out, Joe," George said, "soon, real soon?"

"I'll admit," I said, "that discovering my new family was a shock. I'm still not over it. I'm dragging a little. I'm not depressed though. You know, I'm not sleeping more than normal. They say that sleeping too much and things like fatigue, and feelings of hopelessness, and worthlessness, and not being able to think straight, those things can be signs of depression, and there's other things like a change in your appetite, losing interest in things you liked before, and feeling guilty."

"Oh, we all feel guilty," Bill said.

"Or sometimes," I said, continuing, "you can have thoughts of suicide or wanting to die."

George sobbed.

"I looked it up on the Internet," I said.

"Let's get back to your father issues, Joe," Esther said.

Her voice barely audible, Mary said, "I get depressed quite often,"

Phil said, "Do you think this is a good time to…"

"Does it last long?" I said.

"Not that long," Mary said. "But if I don't keep focused on other people and their problems, like praying for my neighbors and the people at the club and witnessing to them, I can fall into thinking about myself too much, and then I get down. And sometimes I can't tell the difference between having a burden of intercessory prayer for others and just feeling bad about myself."

"How confusing for you," Esther said.

"You just have to keep busy," Bill said. "I sold twenty grand worth of furniture yesterday."

"How about you?" I said to Esther.

"Don't be silly. Depression is only a state of mind. Let's get back…"

Phil jumped in and beat Esther to the punch.

"So, Joe, tell us more about your father," he said.

Mary swallowed hard and said, "Yes, Joe, tell us about it."

"It looks like he was part of a hippie gang in the old days, and so was my real mother, but after she had me, which my dad didn't know anything about, she married some rich guy and left me with my Aunt Margaret, but the rich guy died a year or so ago, and then she decided to let me and dad back into her life. And now she and my dad, who is the senior pastor of this church, as you all know since it's your church, too, got married; they're on another holiday now, leaving Associate Pastor Bernard to run the show, and now I'm rich because of my mother's dead husband, though I guess he would have been my stepdad had he lived. But if he had lived, I probably wouldn't have known a thing about him, or any of them. The good news is he owned a big hotel chain and now I'm loaded."

"So how do you feel about that?" Phil said.

"I like being loaded," I said.

"No," Esther interjected, "how do you feel about your dad?"

"Don't you mean," Phil said, "how does he feel about his mother?"

"His mother was simply a victim of our male dominated society," Esther said. "He has father issues, not mother issues. He had a mother, if I understand rightly, his Aunt was his mother. It's a father he didn't have. We can't blame-shift his troubles onto his real mother, who was blazing a trail for women's equality. At least she gave him life."

George said, "We'll probably never have kids for sure now."

"I'm glad she had me," I said. "Although, I've caused a lot of trouble for my siblings. Pen resents me, I don't know why, maybe for complicating her life, or maybe because I'm getting a share of the money, I don't know. Or maybe, since she's my stepsister but she was adopted, there's some sexual tension...."

"Don't you think we should get going on The Prayer of Jabez?" Bill said.

"...an' that," George said.

"I don't mind opening up some more if that would help the group," I said.

"So, continue?" Esther said.

"It's not about my father, or my mother, it's about my meaning in this life, but not about my eternal meaning which is decided."

"Don't be too sure," Bill said.

"I'm searching for my meaning here on this planet," I said.

"You have to narrow down your calling," Phil said.

"What are your spiritual gifts?" Mary said.

"What do you need spiritual gifts for?" Bill said. "That's why we've got a pastor."

"No, the church is moving away from that pastor-centered model," Phil said. "And that means we all need to discover our ministry gifts."

"That'll never work," Bill said. "Nobody in the church really knows their gifts, never will. There's nobody going to tell us what they are, either."

"What's the point of it all?" George said.

"We pay the pastor to do the work," Bill added. "Why else would we pay him?"

Esther said, "And we're here simply to support the pastor and help him run the church."

"You've been on the Board since the very beginning, haven't you?" Phil said.

"Yes, and I make it my business to support the vision of the pastor. Now and then, when some of us on the Board disagree with the pastor's direction, well, we make some adjustments for the good of all. You see? Leadership at work."

"I was never sure," Phil said, "why you didn't start your own homegroup."

"We like to mix with the people," Esther said, "and show that we can be submissive to others, too."

"We're just like you," Bill said.

"Do you want me to open up anymore, or are we done?" I said.

"You'll fix it, won't you, Joe," George said.

"We do want to get to know you better, Joe," Phil said.

"Yes," Mary said, "we like to get to know those who are relatively new to the church, so we can make them feel welcome in our church family."

"And you, Mary, and you, Phil, are doing a fine job," Esther said.

"Exactly," Bill said.

How was I to love these people? Scripture said I was supposed to. We were supposed to love everybody. But I'd noticed lately some of the people outside the church seemed way easier to love than those inside. And was our opening up to each other going to bring us any closer together? And what if we didn't like what we opened up? Or maybe that was the kind of growth we were looking for, the kind where you overcome and forgive the ugliness we might find in each other. Who knew? But I did know one thing for sure; we were to do it all in love.

"Don't we need a license to do this sort of thing?" I said.

"No, that's the beauty of it," Esther said, "our lives are in each others' hands. Exciting, isn't it?"

"I thought our lives were supposed to be in God's hands," I said.

"It's the same thing," Esther said.

"Let's do a Jabez chapter," Phil said, taking charge.

"Why can't we study a more current church fad?" Bill said. "The Prayer of Jabez is old hat now."

"So, let's begin," Esther said, ignoring husband Bill.

We began, and we grew. With our futures more secure than ever, Phil, in an attempt to keep the peace, asked Esther to close in prayer. Humble Esther granted his request. First, she bound prosperity to us all, and then she bound our wills to prosperity, and then she bound our wills to the will of the church vision, and then she loosed prosperity into our lives and then she loosed our lives into prosperity. She finished with the grand finale of binding each one of us to one another, and then she bound our wills to the will of the church leadership. She then loosed us to go home. Phil thanked her for her tireless and selfless dedication to the church body and said we were privileged to have her and Bill in their homegroup. Mary didn't look so sure of that.

"Let me know as soon as you know anything, Joe," George said on the way out.

"I will, George," I said.

"Sorry about your childhood, Joe," George said.

"Thanks, George, I didn't know you were listening. It wasn't so bad. It's finding out that it was worse than it was that's the hardest."

"Don't worry, Joe, you'll find your meaning."

"I think I have, although some think I'm in denial."

"I'm counting on you, Joe," George said, "…an' that."

CHAPTER ELEVEN

The morning came early in my penthouse office. I'd decided to spend the night there instead of interrupting Aunt Margaret's evening with her suitors. It was 6:45, and outside the grey day loomed. The city would begin to stir in another hour, the city where the almighty dollar called the shots for the half-a-million or so citizens who shuffled their way through their desperate lives. I knew. I'd seen it all. Sure, I hadn't quite seen everything, but I'd seen enough to know that life was tough, no matter how your strings vibrated. And sure, there were exceptions to the norm, there were those whose strings vibrated a little faster than the rest of us, vibrations that attracted more of the doh-ray-me to themselves, and sure there were those whose strings were born into a life of ease, but most of us had just been strung along, and played by the culture that made us. We vibrated to the tune of the Man, or at least, the others did. Not me now. I had been liberated by dough, enough dough that I could play my own tune, vibrate the way I wanted, and right now, I wanted to go downstairs and mingle some coffee-and-donut strings with mine.

Leaving the fold-out couch's blankets in a heap, I reasoned that Pen could deal with it when she came in, since that's what I was paying her for. Singing in the shower, I reflected on Al and George and the whole mess. I knew I needed to make a dent in that case before I volunteered for Spelunker boot camp. It was the least I could do for George. He needed to be put out of his misery, one way or another, and I was committed to see that he was.

Toweling, I decided I needed to put the tail on Al again, and see if she would make a slip and lead me to her other life, if in fact she had another, and what chick named Al didn't? Dressing, I remembered that "chick" wasn't too appropriate these days, even for a private detective, but then there were the Dixie Chicks, who had named themselves that, although you wouldn't have expected Chicks, from Dixie or not, to have challenged the Man. Walking out the door and setting the alarm, I hoped Al would oblige me by leading me to the truth. Riding down in the elevator....

"Ground floor, please, Ben."

"Yessir."

...I wondered if the jelly donuts would be fresh or left over from yesterday. Watching the elevator light flash L for Lobby, and feeling a little queasy from the ride down, I wondered if claustrophobia was an issue with those Spelunker scum.

Slurping my triple-triple and loving my donut, I wondered how long I had before my diet killed me. And then I caught myself. Negative thoughts again. Mornings were usually a negative time for me, and they went slow, the way life could go slow when you slept alone and lived alone, and your family and your church family and the people you met were only islands of otherness on your journey, the wife a dream, the kids only outlines, their number vague.

Outside, the morning sludge had settled over the city. The coming spring was hard to see. My joie de vivre had gone missing. Most people in the new millennium had lost theirs, too. There were some who never had it to lose, and there were some who had never even heard of it, and had no use for the French, either. As for me, I had more of it in the old days, when I was poor. There was a lot to fight for then. But now I was becoming cynical, because reality wasn't warm and fuzzy and comfortable now that I was rich. Life wasn't the way I'd expected it to be. Far from it. The world continued to be hard, the way the world could be hard when the rich got rich—the way I was now—and the poor got poorer—the way I was before,

while out there in the bowels of the city the have-not suckers continued to play the game. I didn't like to think of them as suckers,
because thinking cynical like that just wasn't Christian. And, as we
all knew, we Christians needed to be a positive influence, not a
cynical one. We needed to be more understanding, not less. In this
Third Millennium world we needed to get along more than ever,
here in America, where the Red states and the Blue states clashed,
which was sad, because the Blue-state world was not so far away
from the Red-state world, since, for some, they were contiguous.
But did the Blues think they knew the Reds? And did the Reds think
they knew the Blues? Probably, but how well? The answer was easy;
they didn't know each other well at all, and the little they did know
wasn't pretty. But did the Reds know the Blues a little better than
the Blues knew the Reds? Or did we know each other about equal,
and was that the real reason we didn't get along, because we knew
each other for what we were, even if it was just a little? It was hard
to figure. The Blues had a bad opinion of the Reds, especially the
Christian Reds, who had in their ranks those Born Agains, intoler-
ant of anything fallen. And then there were the Reds, who thought
the only good Blue was a repentant one. Maybe we did know each
other just enough, just enough not to get along. But I, Joe LaFlam,
had volunteered to work among us all, and maybe, just maybe,
straddled on the fence, I might become an ambassador of peace for
both. And after I eliminated the Spelunkers, I would have a fighting chance to work for good. But the Reds and Blues knew nothing about the Spelunkers. They knew a little about each other, but
they didn't know anything about the Spelunkers. But that was okay
for now, because the Spelunkers were my job. I'd been entrusted
with a mission, and for the sake of the Blues and the Reds and all
those around the world who loved to breathe free, I had to stay the
course. I wouldn't let anything get me down, not even the spring
smog that sprang from our own greedy speed and smothered us in
despair. I had to stay up, on top of my game, for the good of us all.

Snapping out of it, I headed to the parking garage to find solace in my Mercedes. Once behind the wheel, I noticed the caffeine had done its work, the way caffeine did its work for all of us, when there was a job to do or a late movie to see, or a craving to satisfy. I was energized now and ready to have another shot at uncovering the truth about Al. I drove over to Starbucks and my destiny with a Strawberry Frappuccino.

Inside the dive, I looked for Al. She wasn't behind the counter. I should have checked with George. She might have had the day off. I asked one of the dames pouring the drinks if she'd seen Al. And just as I suspected, she wasn't in today. It was a definite sign that I needed to skip the Frappuccino. I headed out the door, ignoring the bitterness of the patrons and their coffee. I was happy to leave. I didn't need their negative strings vibrating in my space right now. There was only so much you could take some days, in the spring, in the Pacific Northwest. That's one reason I had my office way up high, where the humdrum couldn't be heard, and that's where I now pointed the nose of my Mercedes, to my office, where Alfred and Abner would be, and where I would be safe once more. Hold it, who was that? Yes, it was, it was Al; she was walking down Main, going my way. What a stroke of good luck—although I didn't believe in luck—that I would just happen to run across her on my way back to the office. It had to be Providential, and I did believe in Providence because it was scriptural. And Providence crossed denominational lines, too. You couldn't find anyone who wore a Christian stripe who didn't believe in Providence. I slowed. Maybe she would lead me to the porno nest this time. The horns honked, but I persevered in my tailing speed. Oh, oh, there she went, she turned in, she disappeared into a doorway. I drove by and read the sign, *SIMPLY SPA*, Massage, Manicures, Pedicures, Facials, Waxing. Providence or no Providence, I wasn't hanging around.

CHAPTER TWELVE

Sunday rolled around again and Church was tough for me to get through. Pastor Bernard was preaching. My step-sisters had missed the service. They had a bad habit of sleeping in. But that worked in my favor today. I wouldn't be tempted to tell them I was about to take the plunge. I knew it was time now to face fear in the face and go under, to mix with the Spelunkers on their own turf. Lord knew it wasn't going to be easy. Even if my sisters had come this morning, I wouldn't have told them anything, or even said goodbye to them for that matter, for their own good. I was on a secret mission. They didn't need to know our family fortune was riding on my mission's success, not to mention the survival of civilization as we knew it, such as it was. Yes, it was easier this way.

I listened to Pastor Bernard, who was savoring his final installment of a seven-week series on Church government. It was all about authority and accountability and relationship. Little did he know that if I didn't nail The Twelve and Thirteen we wouldn't have any Church government. We wouldn't have any kind of government but the Spelunkers. But hold on, that wasn't right. God knew all about evil in the world. In fact, the anti-Christ system fell right into God's plans. So, maybe I wasn't supposed to stop them, maybe I was really supposed to go along with them to be part of God's plan. No, that wasn't right. I was supposed to fight against them. I wasn't supposed to join them. But, this time around, it looked like I needed to join them to defeat them. Okay, so I was going to join them to defeat them, and save the family fortune and the world from the evil rule of the anti-Christ. It seemed like too much for one man to take on. But I had to try. Or maybe this wasn't the real anti-Christ system this time, maybe this was just a warm-up, and once I exposed and defeated them we would have a lot more time before the real one came along. Who knew?

Pastor Bernard summed up his series, saying, "God's government is coming to this planet. His government is coming to the church, and all man-made authority is going to be eliminated. The King is coming to rule the world, and all human corruption of authority is going to be removed from the world. We need to come into line with Him, or we will go up in flames, like the wood, hay, and stubble."

Pastor Bernard was on fire today. But his sermon was no help to me. I was a detective first, and I had an obligation to my client, and to my family. If I'd known how to hear clearly what God was saying, I would have been off to the races. But my hearing was dull. Why was that? I only hoped I wouldn't have to take the 666 Mark. The question was would I be able to join the Spelunkers without swearing allegiance to the Beast? And if once sworn, just for the sake of my mission, could I be unsworn, or would it be too late then, would I be drawn downward into the depths of evil, unable to rescue myself from my mission? No, I was stronger than that. I would stay on course. I was a Christian detective, on the side of good, and if I got the breaks, I would prevail. It was okay, of course, to get the breaks. They weren't the same as luck and had nothing to do with gambling at all. But maybe they didn't have a Mark, and they only did some weird hand-shaking, and they only swore a few harmless oaths, and maybe they just did things like wear their underwear inside-out. That was okay. There was no law against that.

"Ya gonna just sit there?" Abner said.

"Huh, oh, I was just thinking."

The meeting was winding down, and some of the congregation were already in the back getting their coffee and donuts, or going up front to be prayed for by Pastor Bernard and the ministry team, while canned music played in the background. Alfred and Abner were ready to go. Abner watched me thinking for a few more seconds and then shrugged and turned and headed in the direction of the donuts.

Alfred said, "I know why you've been stalling. Tell me you're not going to do it."

"What?" I said.

"They'll eat you for breakfast."

"Any other ideas?" I said.

"Sure, let's forget about the whole thing. Maybe they won't touch your family's business."

"Do you believe that?"

"No, but what you're planning to do is suicide, one way or the other."

Pastor Bernard left the altar and came to say hello. Alfred nodded at Pastor Bernard, turned, and went up front to receive prayer, probably for me.

"How's business?" Pastor Bernard said to me.

Pastor Bernard had a strong interest in business. But who was I to judge?

"Slow," I said, not wanting to spill the beans.

"So there's not much business?"

There he was with his business fixation again. So what did I have to lose?

"Actually, I've got a case, The Case of Twelve. All I have to do is join the Spelunker underground, expose and defeat the Twelve and then Thirteen, aka Maitraya, save our family's fortune, and save the world."

If you couldn't tell your pastor your life's challenges, who could you tell?

"But don't tell anyone," I added, "especially my new mom and dad."

"You know it's Jesus who does the saving; that's not your job."

"Of course it's my job. I hung out my shingle, and the case won't go away. It seems like it's my destiny."

"How is your family's fortune tied to this?"

"If I don't cooperate, the fix is in. Fortune gone. But don't tell them. And if anything happens to me, don't tell them I did it for them."

"You might want to weigh your choices carefully, Joe."

"Thanks for your interest," I said.

"That's my job," he said.

I left him there, my Pastor Bernard, full of advice. Who knew if I would ever see him again? Of course, I would see him on the other side, but would I see him again in the land of the living, that was the question? And would I see anybody again? I looked around at The Church of the Manifest Presence, my home church now, a church of Charismatic believers. But who were we really? We now had a new building, in the suburbs. My rich family had seen to that. No more street church. No more feeding the poor on a regular basis. The congregation had grown to five-hundred, and the building was designed to hold five-hundred more. No more hall downtown shared with the Girl Guides. The church was on its way up. I couldn't help but wonder how much of it was wood, hay, and stubble.

On the way home to see Aunt Margaret, I dropped Alfred and Abner off at their shared condo.

"See you at the office tomorrow, right?" Alfred said.

"Right," I said, and gave them both a wistful look.

"Don't do it," Alfred said, and then he slammed the door of my Mercedes limo.

I drove home perplexed. Why didn't these people understand? Why did they always have to push me and test me? Why couldn't they just accept the fact that an automobile like this one didn't need its doors slammed? And, of all people, Alfred should have known better. This wasn't an old beater, like the ones I used to drive. This was high class and needed to be treated that way. I made a mental note to admonish Alfred, if, in fact, I ever saw him again.

CHAPTER THIRTEEN

Sunday afternoon with Aunt Margaret was slow and hard to bear. I had to look normal, so she wouldn't sniff out anything. I sure wasn't going to let her in on the fact that I was about to risk my life to save everyone's bacon. Dinner was a labor, too. I sat staring into it. I didn't have any heart for it, even though she'd cooked one of my favorites. She'd made it under protest, insisting it wasn't a real recipe. First, you boiled the potatoes, lots of them, while you browned the hamburger in a frying pan, and at the same time you diced an onion and let the chunks soak in vinegar—malt or apple cider—and then you boiled about two cups of water to stir the powdered fake-gravy into. When the potatoes were boiled, firm not soft, you drained some of the potato water into the browning hamburger and turned up the heat to a boil, and then you drained the rest of the water into the sink. Then, you added the two cupfuls of fake gravy to the simmering hamburger. Next, you pearled the potatoes for a few minutes by covering the pot with a dishtowel. Then, you got a big bowl, not a plate—the bowl kept the heat in—and you dumped the potatoes into the bowl, not too roughly. When the hamburger and gravy were boiling nicely, you poured the mixture over the potatoes. On top of that went the onions, including the vinegar. Then, of course, you could salt-and-pepper to taste. It was delicious. But not today. The dish just seemed ordinary today.

"Are you not hungry, dear?" Aunt Margaret said.

"No, I'm not, but you cooked it perfectly," I said.

"There was nothing to it."

I knew Aunt Margaret resented now having to eat it, since I wasn't hungry, and I was the one she'd made it for. She examined a chunk of potato on the end of her fork and then dropped it back onto her plate.

"I don't suppose there's any sense forcing yourself," she said.

Then she proceeded with her arranging habit. She separated the potatoes, the onions and the hamburger into neat sections, the gravy being exempt and free to mingle, and then she ate from each pile in turn, keeping them all even. She finished off with one last forkful of the combined remaining piles, knife assisted. The sorting was always noisy, but she seemed to enjoy it.

"I'll be away for a while," I said. "I'm probably leaving in a day or two. I'm waiting for a call."

"A case?" she said.

"Right."

"Women involved?"

"Right."

"You know you haven't had much success in that department."

"I'm thinking of taking a vow of celibacy," I said.

"You think about it, dear."

"What do you mean?" I said.

"I mean, maybe you should just think about it," she said.

"I'm going to my room," I said. "I'll be there for the rest of the evening."

"You know best, dear."

I felt safe in my room. I needed the security right now, considering what I would soon face. Once I was under, I knew I would be under, and that would pose more than a few challenges. How was I to expose them, and to whom, since most of the powerful, strategic players in the world also belonged to the Spelunkers? I couldn't kill them all. I couldn't kill any of them. Everyone knew why by now. Dilemmas, always dilemmas, but that's what the life of a detective was all about, that and fighting for the underdog. But

who was the underdog in this case? Was it Sissy? If she really was
the underdog, then I needed to defend her rights, although she only
hired me to find Dano and rescue him. But why hadn't she told me
the Spelunker who'd made off with Dano just happened to be her
sister Crusty, and that she was her twin sister, and that her Papa was
one of the Twelve, a Spelunker in word and deed? No, I needed to
have a little interview with my client before I headed underground.
Alfred and Abner would have been useful in that interview, but now
I couldn't take the risk of including them. They might try to stop
me. I had to see Sissy alone, and see which way her needle nose
would point.

The meet was simple. Sissy and I came face-to-face on the
waterfront, where there was freedom to talk from here to eternity
without the unknown's snooping eyes and ears spying on us. The
shrieking seagulls swooped, the frothing wavelets lapped, and the
brisk wind promised rain from the approaching, lowering clouds.
Sissy was somber in black, except for the scarf, a stunning celebra-
tion of buttercup that spilled out from her raincoat and splashed
up to her throat, flashing wittily at both her yellow eyes. Her black
tam sat side-saddle on her slick mane. I'd also come dressed for
the occasion. I wore a brown tweed jacket and a silver sport shirt
open at the neck, revealing a new white T-shirt. My faded jeans projected a devil-may-care attitude that sobered abruptly at my brown
brogues. My blue fedora topped me off. We talked nose to nose.

"You might have told me she was your sister," I said.

"I wanted to see how good you were," she parried.

"Oh, I'm good, alright. So good that I'm going underground
to root out your boyfriend at the risk of everything I am, or ever
hope to be. I'm so good that I'm going to be celibate for the sake of
humanity. That's how good I am, sister."

"Please call me Sissy. I much prefer my nickname. Sister is too formal sounding."

"Sorry, Sissy."

"But do you think you can do it?" she said.

"Sure, I can find him, but what makes you so sure he wants to be found?"

"She's got her evil nails sunk into his brain. Get him away from her, and my Jake will come to his senses."

"That's not a nice way to talk about your sister," I said.

Sissy captured me with her yellow eyes and whispered, "She's a real witch, you know."

"White or black?" I said.

"What?"

"Oh, right, never mind."

So, I had found out what I wanted to know. I was relieved in a way. Sissy was genuine. She had a true hatred of her sister. She really hadn't been trying to set me up. She'd come to *Bell, Booker, and LaFlam* only by chance.

"What about your Papa?" I said, baiting her a little. I had to be sure.

Her head bowed a few degrees. "He's always taken her side," she said. "It's never been fair."

I knew what she was saying. Life wasn't fair. It didn't matter who you were; fairness seldom played that way. But Christians weren't supposed to get involved in all that. Sacrifice was essential to the faith, and I intended to keep up my end.

"Fair is fair and foul is foul," I said.

"Ahh, Macbeth," Sissy said.

"Right. And if I hadn't taken a vow of celibacy, and you hadn't known your Jake, well, who knows?"

"Who knows?" she said, sniffling a bit in the breeze, and then she, laboring, wheezed, before adding her insight. "Who knows what might have happened?"

"Yes, who knows?" I said.

During our talk, the clouds had scudded across the bay, driven by a foolhardy wind that now slammed them into the mountains. The first drops began to hammer down.

"You better get out of this weather," I said.

"How am I to know how your mission is going?" she said.

"I'll get word to you somehow. Have you got a cell?"

She handed me her number on a card.

"I trust you, Joe," she said, and then she turned and bounded for the cover of her distant glistening BMW, her dainty feet scampering, her white calves splayed as she went, like her legs were tied together at the knees.

Seeing her go, I couldn't help but wonder if I would ever see her again, or for that matter, but wait, there they were, the two of them, Alfred and Abner, hiding behind the rest rooms. So, they'd tailed me. Well, there was no harm done, and I did appreciate their loyalty to me, their mentor. I knew I would be able to give them the slip before I went under. And then I wondered if I would ever see them again. They were my true friends and disciples, not to mention brothers in the faith, even if they were each old enough to be my father. I felt a heavy tug on my heart at the thought of leaving them behind. But such was life. And no, life wasn't fair.

I pretended not to see them and headed in the direction of my silver rocket. The rain weighed heavy on my memories, on my perception of self, and on my fedora. Where was I going, and would I never come to the end of myself? Where did I begin and the others leave off? Where were their boundaries, and how much of them was part of me, if any? I would soon find out the answer. Not the answer, of course, to how much each one of us was tied to the others, but the odds were good that I'd find out where my end was. That is, would my descent into Six, or whatever number in Twelve I might be, end me? Seven was a better number, or Eight even. But there was something about Six that reminded me of failure. And was there a chance that instead of assigning me a number they might allow me to choose my own? No, even I knew that self-numbering might lead to disputes over pecking order, and they were certain to know that, too. Allowing the numbers to pick their own would be a recipe for trouble. So, I was resigned to be Six, if that was who I was.

But if I was Six, and of the Twelve, and under Thirteen, that meant the rest of the world's population were digitized, too. Who was number one billion and two, for instance, or three thousand and seven? And who was keeping track? I knew the answer. We all did. Computers were keeping track. That was the easiest way to number us all. But it was obvious that some numbers were going to be more equal than others in the grand scheme of things under the rule of the Spelunkers and Thirteen. Sure, they would no doubt talk about equality. Everybody would be equal in the New World Order, except for the elite, of course, and the super elite, and way above them would be the Twelve, and of course Thirteen. Everybody but them would be equal. The masses would be sentenced to drudgery in the elite's control game, all in the name of peace and security. Well, I wasn't going to be a drudge for anybody, and I didn't plan to be one of the elite, either. I was going to make sure America stayed the way it was. Canada was a good place to be from, and except for small differences, such as Canadians being apathetic and polite and Americans being litigious and pushy, we were pretty much alike. But when push came to shove, America was a better place to be from, because apathetic and polite private detectives just didn't make it in this business.

CHAPTER FOURTEEN

I took another day to think it over. Sure, you could think tough and talk tough and look tough before you stepped into the ring, but sometimes you needed to take a little more time in the dressing room to make sure your courage was on straight. Say what you wanted about the Spelunkers, they weren't stupid. They wouldn't have gotten this far in trying to take over the world if they couldn't smell a committed Christian when they saw one. I would have to keep my beliefs hidden way down deep if I was going to fool them into believing I would fall for being a ruling number, a number somewhere between one and twelve, serving Maitraya. But then when I thought about it, I'd had a lot of practice keeping my beliefs hidden. We all had.

I felt I needed one more homegroup under my belt before I faced death. Okay, so I was stalling again, but procrastination wasn't a bad thing when it had a purpose. I needed to see how George was doing, and to see if we, his caring group, might be able to help him through his trial in some way.

I had chosen to spend my day lounging in bed, reflecting, though I wasn't depressed in any way, and once again, I decided to skip dinner with Aunt Margaret. It was becoming a homegroup night tradition. She was kind and accepting of my decision, except for her reference to that movie again, about the guy who had some trouble with fast food poisoning. I thanked her for her concern, and reminded her that my eating habits were no longer her responsibility. She reminded me that I ate at her table every day, and did I want to continue? I then assured her I appreciated her daily effort, and that I would try in the future to be more picky about where and what I ate.

I made it to homegroup on time, but I was too full to eat my regular helping of jelly donuts. We were all present and accounted for, but tonight the group was hushed. I noticed George was holding onto himself. I honored his space, found my chair, and sipped my cola. The others chatted in low tones around the refreshments' table about church matters. I felt like an outsider. Then they came and sat down.

"Well, let's get started," Phil said.

"Yes," Esther said. "It's time to begin."

Mary frowned at Esther's boldness and then salvaged her face with a crooked smile. They took their seats.

"Well, to begin with, Joe," Esther said, "did you find anything out for George?"

"No, he didn't," George said.

The group raised their eyebrows at me.

"I tried," I said, "but whatever Al's into is pretty hush-hush."

"You'd think if it was pornography," Bill said, "everybody would know about it. I mean I—"

"How many cases," Esther said, rescuing husband Bill, "have you investigated so far in your illustrious career?"

Esther was just being unkind now.

"I told you before, I don't do divorce cases," I said, avoiding her question. "I only did this one to help a homegroup brother."

"Well, you haven't been much help so far," Esther said.

I wondered where Esther's hostility was coming from.

"You're not being very kind," I said.

"Whatever do you mean?" Esther said. "I'm simply here to protect everyone's best interests, especially George's at the moment. I'm sure you are an excellent detective in your own right, and you will eventually find out what Al is up to."

She was buttering me up now. I hated to have a bad opinion of a fellow groupmate, but there it was. She was pretending to be kind, and there wasn't a blessed thing I could do about it. She was a Board member, and that made her an Elder in the church, and I wasn't even an official member yet, even though my dad was the senior pastor.

"How well do you know my dad, the senior pastor?" I said.

"Well enough to know he's on holidays again," Esther said.

"It's not Joe's fault," George said. "He's done his best. He probably shouldn't have taken the job, since he doesn't take these kinds of cases. That's why it's not going well. It goes against his principles... an' that."

"Thanks, George," I said, "but I'll get to the bottom of it yet."

"I've been wondering," Phil said, "do you think we should be discussing this kind of thing at homegroup? Nobody seems to be helped by all this talk, least of all George."

"I agree," Mary said.

"I'm sorry for taking up all the group's time," George said.

"You're a precious member of the group, George," Esther said, "and your needs are important to me."

"And to me, too," Bill said.

I wondered how Esther got on the Board. And then I realized that it was obvious. I knew how she got there; I knew how she got anywhere she wanted to go, but what was her motivation? That was simple, too. Power. She wanted power, power for its own sake. Well, I wasn't going to cooperate.

"We all care about you, George," I said.

"I didn't mean we don't care about you, George," Phil said.

"No, we certainly didn't," Mary said.

"We can talk about it if everyone feels the need," Phil said.

"Pornography is everywhere," Bill said. "It's hard to ignore. Remember that article you read, honey."

"Yes," Esther said, "the statistics are grim. A large percentage of pastors are visiting pornography websites regularly. Too much time on their hands."

"The stress of the job, too," Bill said. "It's an escape for some."

Mary winced at Bill's candor.

I sensed Esther and Bill were enjoying the statistics too much. I wondered why, and then hoped my conclusion was wrong.

"Why are you bringing this up?" I said.

"Don't worry," Esther said, "we know your dad's a fine man."

"Yes, he's on the up-and-up," Bill added.

"I can sympathize though," Esther said. "He's getting tired, and getting older. He needs more holidays now, more time off, the job is so, so demanding, and I wouldn't be surprised if he steps down and lets Pastor Bernard take the helm."

"Has he ever told you that's his plan?" I said.

"Is that a detective question?" Esther said.

"Are we gossiping?" George said. "We're not supposed to gossip…an' that."

I admired George's bravery, standing up to Esther, although, in his current life state, what did he have to lose?

"No, we're not gossiping," Esther said. "We are simply discussing our pastor's situation so that we can make it a matter for prayer."

"He's never mentioned anything to me about retiring," I said. "But I haven't talked to him that much yet."

"Oh, that's right," Esther said, "you don't know him that well, do you?"

"It's the father issues," Bill said.

"That's right," Esther said, "you mentioned last time that your father issues are the reason you became a detective, didn't you, Joe."

"Would you like to work through that?" Phil said, reasserting his leadership and helping Esther at the same time.

"I don't know that I actually have any major father issues," I said.

"I know I don't," George said."

"We all need to recognize certain facts," Esther said, "deal with those facts, and then let them go. Like your dad, Joe. He knows it's time to step down, and now with your mother's money, he'll be able to do it gracefully. Do you see?"

I saw alright. No wonder my dad needed a holiday.

"Well, George," I said, "is there anything we can help you with?"

"No, I'm good, Joe, you're doing your best, and that's all I can ask for…an' that."

"So," I said, "let's get into another chapter of Jabez?"

"Phil's the leader," Esther snapped.

"That's what I thought," I said.

We finished another chapter of Jabez in relative peace, and then Phil asked Esther to close the meeting in prayer. She began by loosing the eyes of every pastor in North America from pornographic images, and then bound them to wholesome ones Next, she released me from my bondage to passive-aggressive behavior, which, she said, taking a moment to editorialize, came from having an absent father. After a pause to collect her inspiration, she released Al from por-nography and lust, and bound her to George, who groaned, which Esther no doubt interpreted as George groaning in agreement. And just in case we were wrong about Al, which she explained to God and everybody, she prayed that Al would be exonerated and George loosed from his neurotic delusions. Then, she bound my father, the senior pastor of the Church of the Manifest Presence, to a happy life of retirement, and released him from the cares of ministry. Then, for good measure, she released my father to a happy life of retirement and bound ministry far from him. This she did, all in the name of Jesus, with whose name she concluded.

CHAPTER FIFTEEN

My limo purred Seattle bound in light rain. Papa had given me the call, and I'd taken that as a sign the timing was right to make my move. The border had been a hassle. They had a few questions. Where are you going? How long are you staying? I saw no reason to say "underground, to join the Twelve, just call me Six." So I settled for saying I was going to a convention for a few days. Suspicious looks, but she let me through. A small fib, so what was so bad about that? What did I care? A grey area, that was all. There was no sense thinking any more about it.

The Interstate was busy as usual, and I got into the rhythm of the freeway. My Mercedes was as good as any of them, and I knew how to drive. I was a former taxi driver, who'd made good, and I knew how to keep up with the traffic, even though I was a Canadian, and I hadn't lived my whole life stateside trying to keep up, trying to measure up, trying to get ahead of the pack to claim my share of the American pie. But wait. In my rearview, I caught a glimpse. There they were. I thought I'd given them the slip at the border, where they'd been about ten cars behind me. I'd figured that by the time they got through, I would be hiding out in Blaine in the rain, that border town where the fluctuation of the Canadian dollar against the American greenback could, from one year to the next, see the merchants either strolling down easy street or lining up at the food bank. But most often, as in other towns, in other struggling communities in this great land, given the general state of humanity, the rain in Blaine fell mainly on the pain.

But my Blaine strategy hadn't worked. Here they were on my tail again. Alfred was good, real good. It was a wonder he hadn't killed me when he was doing the Spelunkers' dirty work. But somebody had been looking out for me, and for Alfred, too, as it turned out. Now I had to lose them again, or they would be doing their best to keep me from my destiny. I put my foot into it. The muffled roar of the engine raised the hairs on the back of my neck and shot adrenaline through my soul. I hit eighty in a flash. Not a feeble eighty kilometers-an-hour, like in Canada, but a solid eighty miles-an-hour, like in America, for I was in America, where the road rose up to meet you and stretched into the horizon of limitless possibilities. But it was no good. There they were a few cars behind in the passing lane. Yes, Alfred was good. And he'd leased a Ferrari, too, and on the company account no doubt. I made a note to set a rental policy in the future. If there was a future. The phone rang; I knew who it was. They had my number. I put on my headset.

"Yeah."

"How about slowing down," Alfred said.

"Ya ain't gonna outrun us," Abner said.

I looked out my window. We were neck-and-neck. Abner smiled and flashed me the peace sign. I slowed to sixty-five. They followed suit.

"I'm doing this alone," I said. "It's the only way. I'm the one they want. You'd only get in the way."

"We're going to watch your back," Alfred said.

"Not if I can help it. I'll lose you before we get to Seattle."

"Seattle?" Alfred and Abner said. "This is the Vancouver freeway."

Abner said, "So why have ya been takin' us on this wild goose chase?"

Okay, so they had me. I'd promised not to live in America in my mind anymore, and now I'd broken my promise. But I needed the escape right now. After all, I was in a tight spot, and I needed the freedom to dream. Oh, why hadn't I been born in America, where

I would be living smack dab in the center of the universe? I had to bust the Spelunkers, if only to preserve the American way of life. But for me, a life south of the border would always be a dream. I'd thought about trying to move south, apply for a visa, maybe apply for citizenship, maybe marry an American, but my family's fortune was in Canadian dollars, so, depending on the exchange rate, I might take a big loss to make my dream come true. And I was pretty sure they wouldn't give me a private eye's license to practice my trade down there. So I was stuck driving down the highway of life, heading for Sixhood, and life or death. And the fact that nobody ever died in my cases was no consolation to me right now. But then again, what if death did come? Sooner or later, we were all handed a one-way ticket to eternity. That was the way it was for everyone, every day, whether we knew it or not. The end might come in a flash, or in an instant, or in the twinkling of an eye. You could buy the farm saving the world or cleaning the eaves on a rickety ladder. You never knew when your time was up, even though you always thought you were the exception and death would never happen to you, at least not before your three-score-and-twenty had run their course, and even then you'd probably think you might cheat the hangman a few years more, if you'd taken care of yourself and exercised and not eaten too much salt, sugar, and fat. As for me, I was almost positive I had arteries the size of sewer pipes, and all that bad stuff just slid through me like blubber on a waterslide.

"Watch where yer goin'," Abner said, breaking into my reverie.

Okay, so they had me. I had to get them off my back.

"I'll meet you at the McDonald's on 5ᵗʰ."

"We will be right behind you," Alfred said.

The restaurant was nearly empty in the mid-afternoon break between the raucous lunch rush and the lonely dinner hour. I eyed the salad section, and then studied the burger menu. McDonald's had changed with the times. Now they had salads to cater to the arteries. Now there was guilt lurking beneath the golden arches.

In bygone days, it was safe here. You could buy and eat grease, and everyone agreed it was good. Now, there were smug salad eaters in the crowd to make you feel dirty. In the old days, the grease-eaters had a silent pact. You ate it and enjoyed it and there were no second thoughts about health.

"Quarter-pounder, fries, and Coke, and supersize it," I said to the young guy behind the counter.

"We don't supersize anymore, sir," he said.

"Well then, as big as you've got. It might be my last good meal for a while."

The young guy thought I was kidding.

"Don't you know that stuff will kill you?" Alfred said, lining up behind me with Abner.

"Ah, leave the boy alone," Abner said. And to our server, he said, "We're all together, gimme one of them Big Macs, some fries, Coke, and make it the big size."

Abner at least was on my side.

"Garden salad," Alfred said in a superior tone, "and a small apple juice."

"Who's buyin'?" Abner said.

We both looked at Alfred. He had to pay for his attitude.

"Yes, of course, why not?" he said.

We sat by the window that overlooked the kids' play area. A young mother in overalls juggled a baby, a toddler, and their burgers and shakes. Life could be tough.

"Ya shoulda waited," Abner said. He dipped a fry in his first of five ketchup cups. "I thought we were a team."

"We can't all go," I said. "It's as simple as that, and you know it."

"No, I don't know it," Alfred said. "There are other ways to do this."

"I'm the one who has to make the choice," I said.

"I've made some bad choices in my time," Abner said. "And this one yer makin' smells like one of them kind."

"You can't trust her either," Alfred said.

"Who? You mean Sissy... or Crusty?"

"Sissy, of course," Alfred said, "she's one of them. She's just having a childish fit to get attention."

"Ya," Abner said, "and she's got them yellow eyes."

"Have you gotten in touch with them yet?" Alfred said.

"You're not getting anything out of me," I said.

"It's not Christian, what yer doin," Abner said. "We're supposed to be a team. There ain't supposed to be no Lone Rangers in the Church."

I wondered where Abner had picked up that piece of information.

"Where did you pick up that piece of information?"

"I kin read, can't I?"

So, Abner had been doing some reading. I was proud of him. But what was my responsibility now as his mentor? I knew I was supposed to agree with the truth, and that living the truth was my duty as his spiritual leader. But then what? What would become of my mission to save the world? And why wasn't anything ever easy?

"Well?" Abner said.

"So, what about it?" Alfred said.

"My explanation might be a little too advanced for you at your present stage of spiritual growth."

"Try us," Alfred said.

"Okay, well you see, it's like this. Sometimes when you're pioneering in new territory, you have to step out beyond the normal boundaries of accepted Christian behavior, in order to get the job done, do you see?"

"No," Abner said, "I don't see."

"I know it's hard for you to understand now, but when you grow a bit more in the faith it will all be clearer to you. Okay?"

"Ya mean, there's stuff to learn that ain't in the Bible, stuff that ya just make up as ya go along?"

"Now you're getting it. It's everyday life."

Abner and Alfred exchanged glances.

Abner said, "Then what's the difference between Christians and ever'body else?"

"You should know the answer to that by now."

"Refresh us," Alfred said.

"We're saved, of course."

I sensed they weren't satisfied with my answer.

"I have to get going," I said, as I finished off the last of my meal. "I've got a job to do."

Abner said, "Why do ya always eat everything all even like that, one chip, one bite of burger, and one sip of cola left at the end, all even?"

I ignored Abner's petty observation, got up and moved toward the door. I dumped my tray's refuse and turned to see if they were about to follow. They continued to sit with their heads down, no doubt continuing to ponder their lack of understanding. Outside, picking at sesame bun seeds, the birds chirped, heralding the coming of spring. I wondered if the bats were singing the same tune.

CHAPTER SIXTEEN

I sat on a bench in Stanley Park. I was dry. The sun was out. The warming pavement steamed. I slipped off my trench coat. What a day! I knew by now that life in this world was about choices. And life in the Kingdom was about choices, too. Like most people, I had a lot of trouble making choices. I usually made the same ones over and over, and, like most people, they were usually the wrong ones. I was no different from the masses. In fact, I was one of the masses. Still, I wondered sometimes if once in my life I might be able to trick God. Instead of doing the same thing I always did, I would do the opposite and fool God. Maybe, just once I might resist the usual temptation. I wouldn't even think about it much beforehand, so He wouldn't catch on, so He wouldn't know what I was up to. It would be my secret. This one particular time, the time of my choosing, instead of following through and making the same bad choice, I would surprise Him, and presto, I'd do the opposite. It would be hard to do, of course. I would have to make it look like I was going to do the same thing I always did. And then, at the last second, I would stop. But because wrong choices were so ingrained, it would be tough to do. Then again, I just knew it was possible to make the right choice at least once. And if I went back to making the same old choice afterward, well, at least I'd have had one victory.

There she was, walking up the path toward my bench, Crusty in blue jeans. She'd come to take me under. She saw me, waved, and then ran and skipped the last twenty yards, like her legs were tied together at the knees. Déjà vu. I stood to meet her. She was glad to see me. I had my doubts about her. She held out her hand. I took it, and we sat.

"You've seen the light then," she said. She threw off her blue scarf, and her blonde hair caught the sunlight and sparkled at no one in particular. Or were her locks sparkling for me only?

"Yeah, I can't keep fighting."

"Where are your friends?"

"I lost them at McDonald's," I said.

"You won't have any regrets. It's a good life, you'll see. You're a World Ruler now; you'll see how it is."

"How's Jake Dano?" I said.

"Oh, Jake's not important. I just did that because Sissy is always on my case. Jake's nothing."

"So where is he?" I said.

"Oh, Papa's got him doing guard duty or something. I think he's guarding the pods."

"Pods?"

"You'll see," Crusty said. "But let's don't talk about pods and Jake and all those silly things that don't add up to a hill of beans in the grand scheme of things."

I was starting to fall for this dame, even though the feminists wouldn't like me thinking of her as a "dame." But as long as you didn't say "dame" that was okay. Or if the word did slip out, which, I had to admit, it had quite a lot lately, then you had to make sure you were in the right company, though that was hard to discern most of the time, because even some Christian gals were likely to take offense. And how could you tell who would and who wouldn't? No, it was better to keep your mouth shut, period, and at the same time try to keep your mind clean of all sexist thoughts.

I decided I'd better say something to Crusty.

"You're my kind of dame," I said, playing along.

"Smooth talker," she said.

Another déjà vu struck me, and then another. Crusty was a lot like her sister Sissy. But twins were like that.

"How'd you get a name like Crusty?"

"Oh, Papa was always in love with the sea."

"The sea...you mean?"

"Yes, Crustacea. Papa named me."

"Is your mother still around?" I said.

"Oh, yes, she and Papa are best friends."

A strange family, but what else would you expect from people who had turned their lives over to the depths of the underworld? Yet, there was something even stranger about Crusty herself. She seemed normal and good. She wasn't sinister. Where was the obvious evil that should have been oozing from her corrupt self? I was beginning to wonder if evil people had just gotten bad press. Yes, there was something wholesome about her, something noble and uplifting. I was excited to sit with her on the bench in the park, like we were two normal people going about the business of courting, the weather today promising us a happy warm spring, a spring of mating and new birth, a spring of frolicking in the...and then I remembered my solid vow of celibacy, that hard unforgiving state of denial I'd committed myself to, more or less. And then there was the case I was hired to solve, and then what about Twelve and Thirteen. Was I losing touch? I had to stay focused. This was serious business. This was no time to allow love to strangle my good judgment. That might come later.

"So, how did an old sea salt end up underground?" I said.

"He got the call, just like you," Crusty said. "He's no different than you are, Joe. You remind me of him a little."

I had a thick head of hair, a trim 180-pound body, and I didn't talk like a snake. But women saw what they wanted to see. To her, I was potential. And sure, I was potent, but I wasn't going to take the fall for her, so she could turn me into a Papa's boy, serving him, number Five, or at least I thought he was number Five.

"Who's your Papa?" I said.

"Pardon me?"

"No, I mean, what number is he? Is he Five?"

"Five? No, Papa's One, second only to Thirteen."

"So, am I Six?"

"That's what we're going to find out," Crusty said.

"How are you going to do that?"

"You'll see, come on. There's a car waiting to take us away from here, to a better place, where you'll be with your own kind. Now you'll never be alone, Joe. And you'll never feel like a misfit again.

Misfit? Where'd she get that idea? I fit in as well as anyone. The "alone" part was sort of right, but everyone was alone. That's the way you were born into this crazy, mixed up world, and that's the way you were going out. Alone. Except, of course, if you were a twin, like Crusty and Sissy, and then you came into the world sort of together. But that didn't mean you'd stay together. Crusty and Sissy were prime examples of that. They were at each other's throats now. In fact, they might have been fighting in the womb and come into the world screaming, not at the sudden shock of leaving the comfort of their nine-month home, but at each other. Who knew? But then again, looking at Crusty beside me—the nimble way she walked me down the path, taking my arm, her sweet smile beckoning to me—who could imagine her delicate hands clutching Sissy's throat, her pretty pointed face happy to watch, as in a mirror, her twin's face turn blue?

"There it is," she said.

I looked for the black limo with the shaded windows, but she was pointing at a yellow Beatle convertible, top down. Papa, wearing a white floppy hat tied under his chin, was squeezed behind the wheel.

"What's he doing here?" I said.

"Papa? Oh, he wanted to come personally. We're one big happy family now. And Papa loves to drive."

So, Papa loved to drive. Well, that was one thing at least we had in common. Maybe he wasn't so bad, maybe we were all the same at the core. Oh, oh, there it was again. I was falling into the maelstrom of deceit. You couldn't just cover over evil with a sporty yellow Beatle. I had to keep my resolve firm. I needed to give my head a shake.

"Why did you shake your head, Joe?" Crusty said, as I climbed into the back seat.

"Oh, I don't know, I guess somebody's talking about me."

"That's burning ears," she said, jumping in beside her Papa.

"Oh, well, then I guess somebody walked over my grave."

Papa's smiling face looked at me in the rearview. "You're one of us, alright," it said.

CHAPTER SEVENTEEN

Crusty and Papa and I were in the cave, eating dinner under the bats. The cave was filled with ambience, all the wrong kind. Papa snapped off a claw and then cracked it open. The lobster fought the sirloin for supremacy in the battle of air odor.

"We want to make it easy for you, Joe," Crusty said.

"You listen to the girl," Papa said. "She knows her stuff."

Crusty teased her parsley garnish and then tossed it into the sweet open hole below her nose. "We really don't have anything against your religion, Joe," she said. "It's all good."

It was all good? Sure. It was all good. That's what they all said. Every self-centered soul, who believed they were a new soul, or a merry old soul, or a coming-around-for-another-go soul, would tell you it was all good. And it didn't matter whether they were dope-smoking souls, or on-a-natural-high souls, whether they absorbed their energy from the crystals hanging off their rearview mirrors, or got their spiritual kicks channeling Elvis, they all had one thing in common: It was all good. But what about absolutes?

"What about absolutes?" I said.

Crusty gave Papa one of those knowing looks that only a daughter can give her Papa, when it looks like the daughter has brought home an imbecile for dinner. Papa, cheeks bulging, nodded at Crusty, waved his next lobster in the air, and then pointed the claw in my direction. Acknowledging her cue to continue, Crusty said, "Look where absolutes have gotten us."

She had a point there.

"The world's a mess alright," I said.

Papa said, "Pa de pepah."

"Swallow, Papa," Crusty said.

Papa swallowed, cleared his throat, and said, "Pass the pepper."

Crusty passed the pepper, smiled at her dear Papa and then continued, "Joe, all religions of the world will eventually be eliminated. Don't you see? The world will be at peace, Joe. Isn't that worth more than your precious religion and the inane notion that there are absolutes?"

"So what will we all worship?" I said.

"For now, anything we want," she said. "We will allow the masses to worship all the projected gods they want to. And those who want to continue on their quest of worshipping themselves will also be allowed to, for a time, and then we will all evolve into worshipping no one at all."

Something told me she had already evolved.

"You can be one of us, Joe, and you can worship whomever you wish, for a time. But you will soon see how foolish you've been, worshipping your absolute God."

I was going to say that my Absolute God was all that was holding this planet together. But I knew they had to eliminate absolutes as a first step toward eliminating my kind. If you went along, fine, if you didn't, you were a goner in the name of peace. All you had to do was love the planet more than the Creator and you were accepted into the earth-loving fraternity. I decided not to make any more waves, or I'd get the boot before I got in.

Changing the subject, I said, "When do I get my number and meet the other numbers?"

"Not so fast," Papa said, "we have yet to determine whether you are one of us."

"So what's next then?"

"Dessert," Papa said. "Chuckles!"

Chuckles entered through the cave door, wheeling a cart. He cleared the table of residual fragments and then covered it again with cakes and pies and wedges and squares. The table was crammed full, like a Southern Baptist potluck before the pastor said grace. Papa smiled at an expressionless Chuckles and then dug in.

"Thanks, Chuckles," Crusty said.

I watched Chuckles leave and then said, "How did he get that scar?"

"It was his own fault," Papa said. "He said he wanted the opportunity to be one of us, a World Ruler, but he failed his first test."

"Takes all kinds," I said.

I wondered what kind of test they had waiting for me, and was it the same one Chuckles had failed? Would I be scarred for life like Chuckles? And if I did pass the test, what kind of diabolical initiation rites would I have to endure? I decided to try again.

"How do we find out if I'm one of the Twelve?" I said.

"Oh, Papa's just teasing, Joe. There's no test for you. We're almost positive you're one of us. But we will know for certain at the initiation."

I knew it. They were going kill me. This whole thing had been a set-up to lure me in, to rub me out the simplest way possible, during an initiation rite. They would make it look like an accident, an unfortunate turn of events. And there they'd leave me, a stalactite-stalagmite sandwich, with me the filling, and a small headline buried on page eleven, *Stalactite Pierces Gumshoe*. The end of it all. And then I remembered. I had to stop these negative thoughts. They were the real enemy. When was I ever going to conquer my mind? The truth was they liked me. Crusty liked me, Papa liked me, and I knew the other numbers would like me, too. Chuckles probably even liked me. And Thirteen, when he got to know me, was sure to like me. There, that was better. I was on top again. What could they do to me? I decided to pop the question.

"Okay, so when do we start?"

Papa scooped a shovel full of ambrosia into his bowl and said, "Now don't get panicky. It's all arranged for tomorrow. You get a good night's sleep, and we'll be ready to go about six in the morning. Any more questions?"

"We're kind of between seasons. What should I wear? Or is this an indoor event?"

"Questions, questions," Papa said, shoveling his dessert in. "You'd think you were a private detective or something."

Papa thought his last comment was funny, and, unable to control his joy, he erupted. Ambrosia filled the air.

Crusty said, "Your clothes and everything you'll need, Joe, will be laid out for you in the morning. Don't you see? Everything's set. You needn't worry about a thing."

"I'm not worried," I said. "I just like to know the score, that's all. I've been around long enough to know you shouldn't mess with the weather this time of year. If you're not dressed right, you know, either you're too cold, or maybe you're dressed too warm, and then the sun comes out, and then you get that creepy feeling when you know you're going to catch a chill, and you know that no amount of rebuking the virus is going to do any good, and then that itch comes in the back of your throat, and then the itch turns into a burning soreness that doesn't go away until the mucous sets in, and then you're clogged for two weeks, blowing your nose, and that's no way to start an initiation, or, for that matter, your life down under, that is if I even survive the initiation. Like I said, I'm not worried; I just like to know the score."

Papa stared at me, lost in thought, a wisp of whipping cream mocking his cheek.

"Oh, you're so sensible, Joe," Crusty said.

I was sensible alright; sensible enough to know I needed a plan. Once I survived the initiation, I needed to know how I was going to bust the whole bunch of them, and once they were busted, who

I was going to turn them all over to. There had to be some straight shooters left in authority in this world. But maybe there weren't, maybe I'd have to start a popular uprising, the masses taking over. There had to be some way. But now wasn't the time to hatch that scheme. Survival was the order of the day, or really survival was tomorrow's day's order. Today, I was okay.

"Pass the broccoli," I said, my confidence beginning to soar.

"It's dessert time, Joe," Crusty said.

I remembered and winked my cute left eye at her.

"Oh, now you're teasing, aren't you, Joe?" she said.

"How about some of that cheesecake, then?" I said. "It looks pretty good."

Papa frowned.

"Just a small piece," I said.

CHAPTER EIGHTEEN

They gave me a cave of my own. Black paper maché decor was just something you had to get used to. The black futon was comfortable enough, but it was hard to sleep in the black light that lit up the white, lop-eared bunnies on my comforter. I would have turned off the light, but any light was better than none at all. And tonight I had a lot to digest. I had a big day ahead of me. A do-or-die day. But either way, I was a winner. If I survived I would be a World Ruler, if I died I would be a shoo-in for heaven. Simple. Heaven would be the easier choice of the two, but, of course, that choice required dying. Although, after the no-doubt difficult dying part, I'd be on easy-street after that. And heaven wouldn't be like this earth, this tormented earth ruled by evil forces that tossed humanity to and fro like a slow clown in a two-bit rodeo. No, heaven would be peace and love and joy, and unlimited possibilities. Apparently evil wasn't required there to keep things interesting. No, evil wouldn't be missed. But life here was a different story. If I survived, I knew that ruling the world would have its complications. Maybe I would play along until I was established in my place, maybe second only to Thirteen, Papa retiring maybe, and then I would be in a position to change things. Then, maybe I could take over the world, Thirteen being removed in whatever way. And with Thirteen gone, I would bring freedom and justice to the masses, with the head number, then being me, choosing to become a much better number than Thirteen, that is, Twelve. No, it seemed too farfetched somehow. I had to stick to my original plan. Continue infiltrating and then bring them down. But how? That was the part that eluded me. I had to trust that the solution would come to me spontaneously, when the right time came, a solution so obvious, that in retrospect no other outcome would have been possible.

Now I had to sleep, but there was no TV in the room, no radio, no books, only the phosphorescent glare of the lop-eared bunnies illuminating my cave. What was the deal about sleep anyway? What did we need it for? One third of your life was wasted, lying there night after night, and for what? There wouldn't be any sleep in heaven. Or maybe sleep on earth was only a shadow of what the real sleep was all about, the heavenly kind of sleep. But then again, what would sleep in heaven be for? Could you waste a third of eternity sleeping? And how long was that? Maybe you could sleep the first third of eternity and spend the last two-thirds awake? But since it was eternity, you might never awake from the first third, unless you could keep track of how long that was, but, since there was no time there, how could you? Yes, I proved it. There would be no sleep in eternity, because if there were, you'd sleep through forever. That meant there wouldn't be any dreams in heaven either, since there was no sleep to be had there. As for sleep here on this earth, we all needed to have it. Right now, I needed some. And maybe I would do some dreaming, too. If only dreams made more sense.

My reflections were startled by a knock on my rock. The paper mâché rock-door opened. Crusty peeked in, her white teeth exploding from her glistening face, her blonde hair alive.

"Are you comfy, Joe?" she purred.

So, that was the deal. More compromise. Well, I had to resist.

"I'm almost asleep," I lied, and immediately forgave myself, knowing that lying was something you just had to do sometimes to preserve goodness. No, she wasn't going to nudge me into the never-ending downward spiral that descended into the pit of human depravity. Not to mention the fact that I was celibate now.

Or was I? "You'll be alright, Joe. Your initiation tomorrow will be wonderful. I just wanted to tell you that. Sleep well."

The rock slid shut.

Well, that was close, I thought. You really had to watch yourself in this line of work, especially on a case that would determine the fate of mankind. I had passed the test. But was it really a test? She hadn't seemed too forward. Only a friendly bit of encouragement. She seemed nice. Maybe she wasn't really that interested anyway. Maybe I had to change my way of thinking. I had judged her really. Just because a person was conspiring to overthrow the nations of the world and bring the planet into submission, didn't necessarily mean she was a harlot. Or did it? Time would tell.

I tried counting sheep, but when I got to six I began to wonder how Al and George were doing. I renewed my hope that Al was on the level, especially for George's sake. But in fact, my hope should have been for Al's sake, since George's spiritual walk was okay, whereas Al, if she failed to see the light, was a prime candidate for the trap door when the world's dust finally settled. They needed my help. I considered asking God to keep me alive, so I would be around to save good old George and his missus. But was offering Him a bribe to save my own skin an acceptable prayer? The answer didn't matter because there was no way I could pray in an environment like this. I needed to sleep. I decided to take a chance, to face my fear. I switched off the black light, and hoped for a brighter tomorrow.

CHAPTER NINETEEN

The bat clock on the wall said six. Morning had come early. I hadn't slept well. My windowless cave was still dark. I flicked on the black light. The bunnies were there to greet me. I sensed a need to reflect, but there was no time for reflection now. I knew I should pray, but before I could focus on my requests, I noticed clothes had been laid out for me on the end of my futon. So, someone had been in my room. I must have slept better than I thought. I was thankful for that. Coffee. That's what I needed to lift the haze that had settled on my mind overnight. Or a Coke, maybe. I could see that my initiation clothes were formal, a black tuxedo and black patent leather shoes. What kind of initiation was this going to be? Not that I had much initiation experience. None, really. Like most people, I'd only heard about what those secretive club-men did in their dens of perverse pleasure. Blood oaths and odd apparel, silly games and cryptic riddles. And what for? So you could succeed in the world and make money, and sell your soul to the buyers and sellers. And this morning, I was preparing for the Cadillac of initiations. Survive and I was a top number, likely Six, and in perfect position to save the world.

I wondered what Alfred and Abner were doing this morning, and my dear Aunt Margaret. Would she be eating her toast right about now? That reminded me. Would they feed me before my ordeal, or was an empty stomach the best way to go? Time would tell.

There was a knock on my rock and then it opened. Chuckles appeared in a flashy three-piece black suit with white luminous pin stripes and a white tie set against a black shirt.

"Going to a wedding?" I said.

"We will see, won't we?" Chuckles said, not amused.

I didn't like his tone. It was foreboding, in sharp contrast with his lively apparel.

"Do you need anything?"

"How about a cup of coffee?"

"That's fair enough. Do you want it black?"

"Cream, and sugar, two spoonfuls."

"Sure, get dressed," Chuckles said, and then he turned tail to fetch my coffee.

"And a Danish," I called after him.

"There will be lots of time to eat later," he said and then added, "if you're lucky."

"How about a Coke chaser, then?"

He slammed my rock. He had an attitude problem. And what did he mean by *if you're lucky*? I didn't like the sound of that. Of course, he might just have been speaking from his own bad experience in his attempt to become a World Ruler, when he'd discovered his number wasn't even in the cards. He was probably jealous, too. Here I was being groomed to be number Six, and all he had to show for his trouble was a butler's job and a perpetual grin. Then again, he did seem to have a servant's heart. Who was I to judge? No, Chuckles was the least of my problems. I climbed into the monkey suit. I looked a lot like Chuckles, minus the pin stripes and the attitude. Whatever was going to happen, it was going to be a high-class affair. Again, I wondered if I would ever marry.

Chuckles reappeared with my cup of coffee on a tray with the cream and sugar.

"Mix your own poison," he said, and then he stood waiting by the door.

Chuckles was beginning to wear. I didn't need his cynicism infecting my morning, a morning like any other, except for the minor detail that here I was on the verge of my destiny in a bat cave under a black light, wearing a black tuxedo and receiving bad vibes from a wannabe who was so far down on the totem pole that he was planted underground. Although, for that matter, we were all underground. I had a bad feeling standing there, facing Chuckles and the door, gulping down my coffee.

Chuckles swung the rock open to signal our imminent departure.

"Okay, it's time to go," he barked, like a ring announcer putting on a show for the paying customers, knowing all along that the fight is fixed.

Searching for a clue to what might lie ahead, I asked, "So how did you fail?"

"A test's not a test unless it's a test," he said.

His puzzling adage sounded almost scriptural. Maybe there was more to Chuckles than first met the eye.

"You don't have any worries, though," he added.

That was good news. Or did he mean I would have no worries in heaven, after they sacrificed me in a ritual conceived to stash more evil power under their belts? Either way, I didn't want to give Chuckles the satisfaction of seeing me scared.

"Are they going to kill me?" I said.

"Just come on," he said, annoyed.

It was clear I wasn't going to get any answers from Chuckles. I followed him through the open rock and headed toward my destiny, and I looked pretty good in my tux, too.

CHAPTER TWENTY

He led me down a winding staircase, lit by more of those neon green candles. I was amazed by how much care the Spelunkers had taken to sustain their interior decorating motif. Although to break up the black and green monotony, I thought the decor might have benefited from a few more sparkling stalactites, which were attached here and there. I made a mental note to speak to Crusty about it.

We arrived, and there they were, four of them, gathered around what looked like a black altar. The room was an average cave size, not unlike a small chapel. No bats hung, but there was a musty odor that infringed on the fragrance of the rose-petal scented incense burning on the altar, or at least I thought it was an altar. I feared the worst. Was I going to be initiated into Sixhood or sacrificed on that altar?

Crusty was ravishing in her red-cowled gown, her yellow locks lining the hood, her nose peaking out, foreshadowing those yellow eyes. Papa and two other men in formal dress rounded out the quorum. I guessed the numbers of the other two were probably Five and under, since I was number Six likely. There was nothing menacing about the scene, other than the presence of the sacrificial altar. Papa, bulging at his tux's seams, nodded at Chuckles, who then left me there and withdrew up the staircase.

Papa, by way of introduction, said, "Two, Three, meet Likely-Six."

"Two, Three," I said, nodding.

"Likely-Six," they said, nodding back.

"Papa," I said.

"I'm One here," he said.

"Right, One, just wondering where Four and Five are."

"You really don't need to know that, but, since you're Likely-Six, I'll tell you, it's their morning to bowl."

I now felt slighted, but why? I didn't even know Four and Five. What did it matter to me if they stood me up at the altar? And why was I at an altar, if an altar this was?

One said, "Let's begin."

"Aye, aye," said Two and Three.

"Oh, joy," Crusty said.

"Do you swear," One said, "to be faithful and true to the Grand Royal Order of the Spelunkers Global, cross your heart and spit to die."

"I do," I said.

"Congratulations, my boy," One said.

"Hear, hear," Two and Three said.

"Oh, joy, oh, joy," Crusty said. "Now I can tell you my secret, ooh, I've been just waiting to tell you."

"Secret?"

"Yes, I'm Seven."

Crusty was Seven? Perfect. But how could that be? I knew from my last run-in with the Spelunkers that the rulers were going to emerge in the form of a collection of Bill Clintons. Surely, she wouldn't want to become a Bill Clinton in the rupture.

"You're not a Bill Clinton type," I said.

"Aha," she said, "there's the part of the secret you don't know about. There's been a change. Now there'll be six Bills and six Hillarys, too, and I'll be the first Hillary."

Diabolical, I thought.

"What will happen to the originals?" I asked.

"They will bow to our rule, or into the vaporizer they go," One said.

So, Crusty would become a Hillary.

"How old a Hillary?" I said.

"The same age as me," Seven said.

"Hmm," I said. "And I'll be a young Bill?"

"That's it exactly," the young, future Hillary said.

What a temptation! No wonder it was so hard to enter in at the strait gate.

"Okay," One said, "now that the preliminaries are over, it's indoctrination time."

"You mean..."

"Yes, you're going to learn the secrets of the ages, and the purpose of our being, and the future of the earth and humankind."

"But how?"

"Seven's going to lead you through," One said.

"Yes," Two and Three said, "Seven's going to lead you through."

One raised an eyebrow at Two and Three, who, not backing off, added, "Hear, hear."

So that's the way it was. I was in, and Crusty-Seven-Hillary was going to take me on the tour of all the hidden mysteries, uncovering for me the reason we were here and the way we would be in the future. Well, that wasn't so bad, and my fingers were crossed when I took the oath, so there was no danger either that I would tumble down the slippery slope of compromise.

"Let's get started," Seven said, "we're off to the Cave of All Wisdom and Knowledge, of things that are and soon will be."

"Hear, hear," said Two and Three.

"When do I meet Thirteen?" I said.

"All in due time," One said, and then he stared down Two and Three, who mouthed, "Hear, hear."

Crusty-Seven-Hillary led me out. I was elated that I was in, but should I have been? That was the question. And was I elated because I would soon have the inside dope on them so I could expose them all, or was I elated at the prospect of Crusty-Seven-Hillary and me exploring the future together? Yes, there was no doubt, I was really beginning to take a liking to this gal.

"Wait up, uhh, Seven?" I said.

"No, you can still call me Crusty, until, oh wow, wait till you hear."

"Crusty," I said, "aren't Two and Three a little, you know?"

"Wait till you meet the future Eight and Nine Hillarys."

"You mean?"

"It's a brave new world. You're not homophobic, are you?"

"No, love the sinner, hate the sin, that's my motto."

"Sin? Oh, don't worry, we'll work that outdated concept out of you in no time."

I wasn't worried, not about any so-called outdated concept, that was for sure. I was holding on to all my outdated concepts. That was the only way I was going to make it through. Sure, I was taking a liking to this gal, but I wasn't throwing my life away for some new concept of humanity that would throw out all the rules in a vain hope for world peace. Sure, I loved the gay folk, but that didn't mean I was going to agree with their lifestyle. And if that meant the politically correct folk would say I was homophobic, well, that's just the way it would have to be. Six wasn't just half-a-dozen, he was Joe LaFlam, and Joe LaFlam was his own man, and a man he was, there was no denying that. But LaFlam wouldn't make waves; he would go along, until the right time, and then he would make his views on the subject known. I then realized that Six was talking about Joe, and, even though Six had some good insights, I refused to become co-dependent on myself. I needed to get back to being just Joe, not Six, too. Yes, I had to resist being Six, who was falling for Seven. A Six was a sucker for a Seven every time. But, I, Joe LaFlam, wasn't going to fall for any one-upmanship. A Six was as good as a Seven any day. Women had been above me all my life, and I certainly wasn't going to be subservient to a higher number now; although Crusty's Papa, aka One, was below me, but he was above me, too, so how did that work? Maybe Seven wasn't higher than Six after all. Well, however it worked, I was going to total the whole order and bring it to nothing, render it zero, cr my name wasn't Joe LaFlam.

CHAPTER TWENTY-ONE

We lay, Crusty and I, each on our own futon, gazing up at the stalactites hanging. The light was dim in the Cave of All Wisdom and Knowledge, where the things that are and the things that soon will be were about to be revealed to me.

"What now?" I said.

"Shh, Joe," Crusty said.

So be it, I thought. Besides, I was enjoying lying there, in the dimness, the two neon-green fake candles gracing the walls, emitting the hope of new life above, on the earth, the good green earth, where justice one day would prevail, where everyone would live at the end of this age in Millennial harmony. And hope was a good thing. But I knew that hope wouldn't be realized like this, lying on my back beside Crusty in this Cave of so-called Wisdom and Knowledge, the place where the underworld's schemes were made known.

"So what's your take on Plato?" I said.

"Shh, Joe," she said again. "This isn't the time."

But what was it the time for, in the dark, here, with lithe Crusty, whose perfume was now wafting by? I hadn't noticed that before. It was nice. I entertained a stray thought, but then caught myself and commanded it to go. I needed to focus up there, past the stalactites, on the cave's ceiling, where the sparkles on the fake rock glinted green. And then it started. The cave lights were snuffed, and the ceiling began to dissolve and open up, and images formed. Had I been drugged? Had they slipped me some kind of mind-altering concoction in my coffee, so my mind would be malleable and my inhibitions erased.

"Hologram?" I said.

"Shh, Joe," Crusty said.

I resumed staring up there, where scenes unfolded of happy citizens frolicking on the good Earth. And then the words splashed forth, The Age of Ages Is Coming, Soon to Planet Earth. And then a Rod Serling type appeared, not smoking, and he fixed me with his eyes.

He said, "The Plan is unfolding as it should. The future of the universe is set. You are the hope of things to come."

Crusty giggled.

"Who's this guy?" I said.

"Shh, Joe," she said.

"Look," the man said, and waved his hand.

He disappeared, replaced by words in black letters floating in a nifty sky blue, THE NEW EARTH UNDER THIRTEEN'S RULE OF TWELVE.

Next, subheadings swooshed in, like supernatural Power Point. The list was vexing: A) *One World, One Us* B) *Networks of Joy* C) *Spaced Conflict* D) *Getting There.*

Then A) flew forward, or down really, since we were looking up, and B), C), and D) fled away with a sucking sound. In my face was One World, One Us, and then the letters dissolved with a whir. In the space above, marching people appeared, about ten abreast from four directions, North, South, East, and West. There were thousands of them of all races and colors, and they were smiling and radiant in their ethnic costumes. It was a splendid sight, full of life and hope, the people of the world uniting, but at the same time, I was alarmed. I could easily see they were heading for a pileup when they all converged in the center. What drama! I winced in anticipation of the mess and chaos that was bound to ensue when they collided. But there was no collision. They continued marching through each other, blending their characteristics. Through each other they went, a smiling, kilted pygmy here, an Asian in a cowboy hat there, all mixed together as one. This was the future, a blending of the races and cultures to form *One World, One Us*. In fact, that's what the swelling voice said, "Here we are finally, the hope of the ages realized. We're all together now. Yes, we're all together now. One World, One Us."

It was a pretty picture to be sure, but, just because the Spelunkers had created clever images of humanity marching into itself and becoming one, didn't make it so. I'd seen *The Fly*—closing my eyes, of course, during the questionable scenes—and I knew you couldn't mess with people's genes that way. Change took time. And time took a lot of time. And for me time was long. People had always told me time just flew by. But time wasn't like that for me. For Joe LaFlam, ages had gone by since he was a kid. And then came his teen years, the ugly-duckling stage that lasted for eons. And then came his twenties and creeping mediocrity for that long, slow decade. And now, in his thirties, the inching labor of seconds turning into minutes, and minutes into half-hours and half-hours into hours and hours into half-days and then ticking into twenty-four hours, and the days thudding by. Oh, the days. And now he was thirty-something and rich, but time stayed the same. Slow. For a long time, he had hoped a wife would come along and speed things up a bit, but hope for that was slim and time long. He thought sometimes that maybe time went so slowly because at night he often replayed the day's events in his mind. Maybe the replays lengthened time, like a clock with a near-dead battery obsessively-compulsively ticking the same second until it finally gave out. But how to stop? How to stop replaying the days. He imagined what it would be like to live sixty more years, into his nineties. Impossible torture. He longed for the rapture but knew he had to solidify his meaning first, no matter how long it took. No, he didn't want to show up there too soon and be asked what he was doing there so early. No, he had to endure, to contribute, to do his time. Time speeding by? What a laugh. He laughed out loud, but who laughed? It had to be Six. There he was thinking as Six again, and I, LaFlam, was being third-personed to death. No, he...no, not he, but I needed to stay LaFlam, no matter how much time there was to think and how long time took. Like now, for instance, the long time it took between A) and B), which now flashed overhead, B) *Networks of Joy*. And that same voice was announcing *Networks of Joy*. And what had they put in my coffee?

"Did you ever see *The Fly*?" I said.

"Oh, Joe. Okay, hold the show, Chuckles."

The green, fake-candle cave lights came up and the ceiling turned back to black.

"How can you go mixing everyone up like that?" I said.

"It's the way to peace, Joe. We can't fight one another when we're all together as one."

"I think fighting is a better solution."

"Oh, Joe, you're funny. You'll see, it'll all make sense soon."

I was beginning to wonder if these were genuine Spelunkers. Maybe they were a shadow group of conspirator wannabes, and I was being set up to be a Six in a half-baked scheme, so that I'd sell out to the Beast and take the Mark, and then it would turn out it wasn't even the real Beast, and I'd been suckered again, another test I'd failed. And why was it always so hard to discern if and when you were being tested? You might think you were being tested in one area of your life, and you find out later you were really being tested in another. But I knew one thing for sure. I wasn't going to walk around with Six engraved on my forehead for nothing. Come to think of it, I wasn't going to fall for any of this. I'd come to find Dano for Sissy; that's what I'd been hired for, and that's exactly what I was going to do.

"How about Jake Dano, can you tell me where he is?"

"Oh, Joe, why do you insist on dwelling on the mundane? Jake's a nobody now."

"Was he ever a somebody?"

"Not to me, Joe. That was all in Sissy's head. Besides, he would have made a poor Six."

"A poor Six? You mean? Where is he now?"

"Oh, Joe, he's long gone. He wasn't entirely honest with us, either. He was spying for the Clan."

"The Clan?"

"It's a devious group of anti-globalists, Joe, that's trying to destroy us. He tricked Sissy, and he tricked me. There, are you satisfied?"

"No, I'm not satisfied. I don't know if I'll ever be satisfied, until my meaning is secure in this crazy mixed up life."

"But, Joe, we are your meaning. You're Six and I'm Seven. The world is ours. What more do we need?"

"I'm sorry. I have a hard time believing I'm a World Ruler when I've never really succeeded at anything."

"Do you have a hard time receiving, Joe?"

"Well, yes. I guess so. I've had all this wealth dropped into my lap from my real mother, and I'm at a loss to know really what to do. And now I've been given another chance for advancement with this World Ruler option. It's too confusing. It wasn't that long ago when I wondered if I'd ever escape the fate of dying destitute in a big city alley."

"Well, Joe, at least your ambition was bigger than dying in a small town alley."

"I suppose, that's something."

"But don't you see, Joe? You have been given these gifts and opportunities because of who you are. You deserve what you get, because you're you. Your money was inherited because you were born to it, and you're a World Ruler because, when you were born, the cosmos was perfectly aligned for greatness to emerge. You're made of Star Stuff, Joe. The right Star Stuff."

"I thought you didn't believe in anything spiritual."

"I don't, Joe. Stars are just stuff. And we're all made of it. Some of us are just made of better stuff."

"But haven't you ever wondered where the stars came from? Don't you think there had to be a first cause?"

"No, Joe, there was only a First Stuff. The stars are just there. They birth themselves out of stuff and then fling out from themselves planets and other stuff. Stuff is the womb for everything, and when you die, you turn back to stuff."

I could see my evangelism effort was going nowhere.

"So Dano's still alive?"

"Oh, of course, Joe. We're not heartless."

So, if she was telling the truth, Dano was still in the land of the living. That was good news. I wasn't alone, and even if I discovered later I didn't agree theologically with Dano and the Clan, and there was a good chance I wouldn't—given the fact that anti-everythings didn't associate with my kind—they could always be converted later. Yes, exposing the Beast made strange bedfellows. So now I had an even greater need to find Dano, if he was still alive, and there was a good chance he was, because Crusty said he was, and because nobody ever died in my cases—yet, that is.

I said, "Okay, sure. Let's get on with the show."

"Hit it, Chuckles," Crusty said.

Chuckles hit it, and the candlelight dimmed. The hologram began to take us through space. Billions of stars flew by. Then, I realized I was only looking at the hologram-saver. The voice announced again, *Networks of Joy*. What followed was stunning. As it turned out, *Networks of Joy* linked people to each other by the next generation of the Internet. Everyone was wirelessly wired to everyone else. So, in addition to having everyone's genes pooled in *One World, One Us*, they were also sharing their daily lives by tuning into each other's experiences through computer-chip, brain implants. *Networks of Joy* brought a new depth to the words, "we met on the Internet." But on the New Net, you didn't just see the other person, not like in the old days when you had a camera on your computer. No, on the New Net you could see and experience their lives through their eyes, their minds, their emotions, their senses. And everyone could do it. You were implanted at birth. You could go anywhere in the world and see how the others lived. And there was no pain in this new world of experiential joy. Everyone was happy being anyone else they pleased. New contacts were made, Internet addresses were exchanged, all on the wireless *Networks of Joy*. Anyone could experience any other they wanted.

"I'd prefer just to be me," I whispered.

"Shush, Joe, I don't want to stop it again."

And on it went. If the medium was supposed to be the message, then the message had become us. We had become the content and the message. No more watching those reality shows. Now we could be in any one of a billion other realities we wanted. We had become each other. And we could date anyone we wanted, too. You just tapped into anyone who had a good thing going. No more marriage. Relationships lasted a few minutes, or a few hours, and then be no more. No marriage, so no divorce. Solved. Life was simple on the *Networks of Joy*. And nobody worked, unless they wanted to. And nobody went to school, unless they wanted to. You could go offline and do your own thing for others to experience or go online for as long as you wanted. No crashes, no viruses, and poverty was no more. Pain was no more. Labor was no more. All the food and the necessities of life were provided. The population was kept at the exact number for Gaia, aka Earth Stuff, to sustain. This Gaia thing was alive with the sound of music, too, vibrating its essence into everyone, and everyone was vibrating to the lives of everyone else, and being everyone else, and life's quest was to be everyone else at least once, and there was no death; your chip crashed when you reached the maximum number allowed for being someone else. And then you were vaporized, your vapors then becoming one with Gaia.

"This is no fun," I said.

"Okay, hold it, Chuckles," Crusty said. "What now, Joe?"

She sounded miffed.

"Well, come on, how boring can you get? Joy, joy, joy, and then you're smoke."

"Oh, Joe, if that's all that's bothering you. That's just for them, not for us. We need to keep them busy, that's all, keep them entertained, while we're doing the important things. And besides, it's not all joy. Just watch what's next. Okay, roll it again, Chuckles."

"One other thing."

"Hold it, Chuckles. Yes, Joe?" She was patronizing me now.

"I thought you said you didn't believe in anything spiritual. So what about this Gaia stuff?"

I had her there.

"You've answered your own question." She was becoming impatient. "Gaia's just stuff, Joe."

So, Gaia was just vibrating matter. There wasn't much joy in that, not that I could see. No, and it certainly wasn't all joy. Who would want to be other people, leading other people's lives, if only for a few minutes? Hmm, there were a few exceptions there, but no, definitely not; we all needed to be kept separate. If God had wanted us all to be one, he would have made us that way. He did intend for us all to be one in Heaven, but then we would also be individuals there. In fact, in heaven we would be who we really are, and for eternity. So, no contest, God wins, Gaia loses. And, for a person in my line of work, there was another big objection to this whole plan. If everybody was "one" here on Earth, nobody would have any use for private detectives. Because nothing would be private, and there wouldn't be any mysteries to detect, either.

"Roll it," Crusty said.

Chuckles rolled, C) *Spaced Conflict*. The atmosphere changed. Joy had gone. The room thundered and explosions blasted, and soldiers, male and female, were blown up and stacked in piles and then vaporized. The women wore pink helmets, the men wore blue.

And then the voice spoke, saying that culling was required every 10 years, and so the Battle of The Sexes was then waged. Men against women. Contingents of troops in the millions from every part of the globe came together to fight in what was formerly Ireland. It was sort of like paint ball, only for real. Lasers and surface-to-surface missiles were the preferred weapons. Sometimes the men would win, sometimes the women. This was programmed into the battle. For one week, the *Networks of Joy* became the *Networks of War*. Everyone in the world was encouraged to experience someone in the battle. In this way, not only was the population kept to a proper Gaia level, but the innate animosity between male and female in the collective consciousness was pacified and the air cleared for another ten years. And then the *Networks of Joy* started back in business again. But I wasn't born yesterday. *Spaced Conflict* would never work. It was impossible to manage the battle of the sexes by programming periodic violence.

Next, D) *Getting There* appeared.

"It won't work," I said.

"Right. Hold it, Chuckles. What won't work, Joe?"

"Programming violence. Hatred and violence just are. You can't control that."

"We," she said, spacing her words, "we can do anything we want to do."

"Joe," I said.

"What?" she said.

"Joe. You always call me, Joe. You didn't that time. Are you angry with me?"

"No, Joe. Of course not. I know you haven't really understood everything yet, but you'll see. I'm sorry, okay, Joe?"

"Okay."

"Roll it, Chuckles," she screamed.

D) *Getting There* again exploded into view, and the voice said, "*Getting There*, this is what it means."

By this time, I really did want to know what it all meant. There was Papa, in his black tux, seated around a table with eleven others, who had black sacks over their heads.

Papa spoke, "You have been chosen to be one of these."

He waved his hand at the black sacks, who nodded on cue.

Papa continued, "We are the Twelve who will rule. These, of course, are mere actors. At this present time, not all of the predestined Twelve have been named, but because you are now watching this, you are none other than a number, between One and Twelve, though, of course, you can't actually be One, because I am One, and you can't be Seven either, it's already taken, and it's not nepotism, because she qualifies in her own right. So, any one of these other remaining numbers you might very well now be, since, as I said, you're watching this. You get my meaning, I'm sure."

Papa was a natural orator. He was gifted and commanded your attention. I understood now why he was One.

He continued, "So how do we get there? I can tell you that it will be neither by the sweat of our brow, nor by some kind of foolish sacrifice, but through science, technology, and the wealth of the ages. It doesn't hurt either that anybody who is anybody on this earth is one of us. Yes, my fellow numbers, we have evolved from Star Stuff slime to Star Stuff sublime. From a single cell amoeba to a vociferous Rush Limbaugh. We, my fellow numbers, have arrived. Timing is the key. And the time is now. The starter's gun has been fired, the green light is flashing, the flag has been waved, the coin has been tossed, play ball has been yelled, the bell has been rung, the whistle has been blown, the ball has been bowled. We need only to look to ourselves now, and to ourselves alone, and be about the business of *Getting There*."

Papa and the black-sacked Eleven then dissolved in a peal of thunder. D) *Getting There* entered from the left, lingered a moment and then exited to the right with a swish. In its wake, subheadings i), ii), and iii) popped up. Next to i) *getting rid of them*; next to ii) *the ascendency*; next to iii) *rule for good*. Then ii) and iii) dissolved with a gurgling sound, leaving i) *getting rid of them*. Next, i) *getting rid of them* exploded with a bang into letter fragments, which a little man in janitor's overalls came and swept away, taking himself with them. The voice said, "The religious zealots, and we know who they are, will be given an opportunity to turn from their narrow ways, and if they refuse, they will have their Star Stuff recycled, no hard feelings. Next, the intellectuals and the academics, and we know who those rabble-rousing intelligentsia are, will be given a chance to recant and dumb down a little, or their high-minded Star Stuff will be mixed again with the earth."

I was thankful I was only threatened on one level, but I pitied Pastor Bernard. He was a Christian and an intellectual. What hope did he have? So, in the long run, it was probably a blessing there weren't that many Christian thinkers around. God had taken the foolish things of the world to confound the wise. That was scriptural and made me feel important. But was I foolish to feel important? Was being foolish good or bad in this case? Or was I wise to feel important because I was foolish. Who knew? Anyway, in the big picture, you didn't have to be both a Christian and an intellectual to get vaporized; you only had to be one of them, a Christian or an intellectual. You were dead if you were either. They couldn't recycle you twice for being both. On the other hand, you had the choice to recant and be saved, but saved to do what? To mix your genes with the rest of the people's and plug into the *Networks of Joy*? What kind of life was that? It was no life at all.

The Flying Through Space hologram-saver appeared again, as the voice continued.

"We'll keep the scientists alive, as long as they see it our way. But, it goes without saying, the anti-globalists will have to go, and the New Ager types, especially the neo-pagans, along with the witches, white and black, and anyone who was known to have waited expectantly for the dawning of the Age of Aquarius. Accompanying them all into the vaporizer will be the romance writers, impressionist painters, and fashion designers. Thus, the world will be cleansed for the rise of the Twelve."

At least private detectives weren't on the hit list, even though they wouldn't be needed in the new world. And, for some reason, there was no mention of mimes. Next, the hologram-saver vanished to reveal ii) *the ascendency*, which melted into a puddle, and then the little janitor came back again and hosed it away. Flying Through Space resumed, as did the voice.

"Up we're coming, we're coming up, and the world will be a better place, a far better place for us."

For us, maybe, but what about for the masses? What about those poor slobs forced to live fragmented lives, not sure who they are, addicted to living the lives of others, and their only hope to delay their inevitable vaporization? What kind of life was that?

"What about the masses of humanity?" I said.

"Chuckles," Crusty said. "Stop, stop again. Now Joe, you aren't paying attention. This isn't about them, it's about us."

"Well, what will we be doing that's so important?"

"Ruling, Joe, ruling. Don't you get it? We'll be in control. We will be ruling the world. The masses need to be kept under control. If we allow them free will, they will continue to hold us back from our destiny. Their ridiculous behavior over the last 10,000 years has kept the elite Star Stuff from evolving. Now we're going to manage them, and as you and I know, they will need managing, because they always find some way to cause problems, which we will have to solve."

"Yeah, sorry, I forgot. It's so easy to lose focus when you're in transition. But why keep the masses around at all?"

"Joe…Joe…Joe…you haven't been paying attention. You know the answer yourself. We need them to rule over, of course."

"Of course, I forgot. And you're sure the devil isn't in on this?"

"Devil, Joe? Oh, I see, you're joking with me again, aren't you?"

I winked at her in the dark and laughed. She giggled and then intoned gaily, "Roll it, Chuckles." The Flying Through Space screen-saver resumed, and the voice continued.

"At the perfect time the Rupture will unfold. The Twelve will emerge from their pods transformed to rule. And Thirteen will rule them all."

"Any popcorn?"

"Chuckles!" Crusty screamed.

"If there's much more of the show left to go." I said, "I wouldn't mind some popcorn, and a cola if you have one. This always happens when I go to the movies. Ever since I was a kid. I would get part way through the show, and then I couldn't concentrate any longer unless I got some popcorn, and maybe a cola. I thought I could make it through, but the "emerging from their pods" part reminded me of fresh popped popcorn. Sorry."

"Joe, we're nearly at the end. Perhaps you could just wait. You are, after all, at this moment learning how we're going to rule the world."

What was the use of ruling the world if you couldn't enjoy the little things? I'd at least learned that much so far on my search for meaning. A Big Mac with friends, popcorn during a movie, your girlfriend snuggling your arm, watching a pre-toddler take her first steps. And even though I hadn't yet watched a toddler take her first steps, I was sure the experience would be precious, fascinating, and memorable. For that matter, I hadn't experienced a girlfriend snuggling my arm either. But I was positive it would be one of those little things that made life worthwhile. Although at this time in my life such an experience would have been a big thing, not a little thing, given my record to date.

"What's the use of ruling the world if you can't have the little things?" I said. "It's the little things that count."

"No popcorn till we're done," she said

"Joe," I said.

"What?"

"You skipped calling me Joe again. Are you angry?"

"Yes, yes, I'm angry. You're being offered your destiny, and all you can talk about are the little things. Come on, Joe, you're bigger than that. You were born to rule. Don't let the mediocre social situation you lived in when you were growing up, and your inept performance in your chosen profession, cloud the view of your future."

"Why are you putting me down and reinforcing my negative thoughts about myself? I'm trying to stop doing that."

"What are you talking about, Joe? The future is nothing but positive for us. You and I ruling the world, that's the future. Forget about the masses, forget about the little things. Do you understand? The stars have determined your destiny. You and I are stellar Star Stuff."

"That's better, much more positive," I said.

"Can we continue now, Joe?"

"Sure, never mind the popcorn. I'm sorry I brought it up."

"Good. We're ready, Chuckles!"

"Joe," I said.

"Right, good, Joe. Chuckles!"

The hologram-saver resumed, and the voice continued.

"And Thirteen will rule them all. Our state-of-the-art gene-a-sizer pods are designed to transform the ruling elite into the ultimate human specimens. Six Bills, six Hillarys. Twelve to rule. Slight variations in skin pigment and hair color might apply."

Flying Through Space then ceased, and twelve white coffin-like pods appeared, ready to heave their contents onto the good earth, which opened up in gashes from beneath, and then the pods shot up and through the gashes, ejecting a Bill on this continent, a Hillary on that one, until all the Earth's twelve jurisdictions had been covered by the rule of Twelve, the rupture ending in triumph.

The hologram-saver resumed, and the voice continued.

"The thrones will then be occupied, and only then will Thirteen, the crème de la Star Stuff, be revealed to the masses."

What an anticlimax. It looked like they weren't going to reveal Thirteen's identity.

Flying Through Space yielded to iii) rule for good, which was encircled by the anonymous twelve human figures, now wearing golden, hooded robes, their hands raised. Then, poof, and the hologram-saver flashed its stars once more.

Next, the voice said in an imperious tone, "The Twelve rule for good."

The stars stopped, and a summary was presented.

THE NEW EARTH UNDER THIRTEEN'S RULE OF TWELVE

A) *One World, One Us*

B) *Networks of Joy*

C) *Spaced Conflict*

D) *Getting There*

    i) *getting rid of them*

    ii) *the ascendency*

    iii) *rule for good*

The words then burst into confetti, and the little janitor man entered with an electric fan and blew the little pieces out of view, taking himself with them. The ceiling faded to black, and the green cave-lights came up.

"Well, what do you think, Joe?" Crusty said.

I was overcome with the depth of depravity the human race could descend to. Here was Crusty, a normal female—just to look at her—and yet she was an instrument of evil, helping to hatch the most diabolical scheme ever conceived. Crusty was a world-conqueror type, a dime-a-dozen really. You could find them under any rock. The only difference between the others and her was that she and Papa were most likely going to pull it off. Unless, of course, I stopped them. I had to find Dano, to see if he had a plan, any plan, to bring their devilish house of cards toppling down, or rather, to raise their seething house of decay up into full view, where the light of day would expose the corruption inherent in any one elite group trying to rule the world. I had to find Dano, or die trying.

"It would have been better with popcorn," I said with a wink.

"Oh, Joe, you are incorrigible."

"What now?" I said.

"The best part, Joe," she said.

We each sat up on our futons. She swung her legs over, and so did I. We faced each other. She engaged me with her eyes. There was love in them. I was pretty sure that's what it was, but I couldn't be positive because I hadn't seen it much. Never, really.

"Best part?"

"Yes, Joe, it's the secret of the Ages."

"What is it?"

"Thirteen, Joe."

"We just heard. We won't know who he is until the Twelve Thrones are established."

"It's not a 'he', Joe."

"Not a 'he'."

"No, Joe"

"Who?"

"Us, Joe."

"Us?"

"Yes, Joe."

"How can we be Thirteen?"

"You're Six and I'm Seven, Joe."

"So?"

"So, Joe, don't you see? Six and Seven make Thirteen."

"Oh."

"Is that all you have to say, Joe?"

"Pretty much."

"Oh, Joe, you don't get it yet."

"No, try me."

"Wait till you hear, Joe."

"Fire away, I'm listening."

"Well, Joe, first we live as Seven-Hillary and Six-Bill until we're stable, and then after a few months we move to the final stage."

"Which is?"

"Are you ready, Joe?"

"I can't wait."

"Now, Joe, are you ready?

"Yes, I'm ready."

"We both go into the same pod together."

"Together?"

"Yes, Six and Seven, Joe, together. Our Star Stuff combined."

The penny dropped.

"You mean our genes will be combined?"

"Exactly."

"Joe," I said.

"Right. Exactly, Joe."

"Bill and Hillary combined?"

"You've got it, Joe."

She beamed as she watched me grasp the depth of the revelation. I smiled back, but I wasn't smiling inside. So, this was the payoff. This was what my destiny dictated according to their Star Stuff game. Well, I wasn't born yesterday. No, I certainly wasn't born yesterday, mainly because time always went slowly for me; it seemed like ages since we started the movie, and time was certainly thudding by right now. So, Six and Seven made Thirteen. It all added up. One body, one flesh, androgynous, and, irony of ironies, permanent celibacy realized. The ultimate synthesis of co-dependence. And to top it off, the whole world would be run by one big Hillbillary. That was some machine. Well, I would have no part of it. I could see now that I'd been looking for love in all the wrong places.

"Who'll be the new Six and Seven then?"

"Is that all you have to say, Joe?"

"Do you always answer a question with a question?"

"Do you, Joe?"

We were squabbling now, but she was still calling me Joe. That was a good sign. I needed time to think, I needed some quiet time to gain proper perspective. *I don't like the plan either,* Six said in my mind. I decided to smooth the waters.

"It was only a technical question," I said, "and since we'll be ruling together soon, I'll have to anticipate these kinds of things."

"Ahh, Joe, I see. Well then, I'll answer, we've got a backup set of Six and Seven."

"What if the backups decide to combine, too?"

"You're really giving this some thought, aren't you, Joe? I'm impressed. Maybe you weren't such a bad detective after all."

"Bad detective?"

She had really pressed a button this time. Not only was she planning to merge me with her harlot self to become the personification of evil, a Hillbillary eunuch Lord Maitraya, she had also shoved a stiletto deep into my self-esteem. It was hard being a detective sometimes. But this was what I had been trained for all those years, watching Cannon and Magnum and Rockford and Beretta.

"Oh, Joe, let it all go," Crusty said. "It's you and me now."

Well, I wasn't going to let it all go. I was going to see myself to the very end being only me, Joe LaFlam, Christian Detective, and I was a darn good one at that. No more negative attitude for me. They would all see the truth about me. The whole twisted bunch of them, or my name wasn't Joe LaFlam. I wasn't going to be wedded to evil for anyone.

What about me? Six said in my head.

You're history, pal, I thought back at him, not unkindly.

"So when do we get it together?" I said, not wanting to tip my hand, but, of course, when I played cards, and that was infrequently, I only played for matchsticks.

"That's my boy, Joe, now you're getting it. Three to six months, tops, and everything will be in place for synthesis, the ultimate synergy of elite Star Stuff."

That was good news. Three to six months gave me the breathing space to find Dano and formulate a plan.

"That's a long time," I said.

"Oh, Joe, now you're as anxious to get together as I am. You just cool your heels, Mister."

"Okay, so what's our next step? I'm depending on you to get me up to speed on all the ins and outs of ruling the planet. And once I'm on top of my game, I'll be able to provide the proper leadership for us both."

"Both, Joe?"

"No, you know what I mean, so I can be a worthy equal. So that we can come together on an equal footing."

"Hmmm," she said. And then she said it again, "Hmmm."

"You mean, hmmm, Joe, don't you?" I said.

CHAPTER TWENTY-TWO

Back in my personal cave, I replayed the morning's show in my mind. Crusty had been content to allow me some down time while I soaked in the enormity of the future. Who did she think she was kidding? Who in their right mind would want to donate themselves to another human being, lock, stock, and barrel? No, co-habitation was not for me. And what would a Hillbillary look like? Besides, the potential for internal chaos was limitless. We'd be living on Prozac for the rest of our life. My only hope was to find Dano, and together we would bring them down. I hoped I wasn't putting too much faith in Dano, a man I'd never met, and only seen a picture of, and could you get along with an anti-everything type? Did we have much common ground? Those questions needed to be answered when I found him. Right now, I needed a clue to where he was

The other question was whether they were going to let me out of here. And was Dano in or out, above or below? I didn't know that either. So that was another question I needed an answer to. I was stuck. And my cell phone had been lost somewhere in my coming underground. Then I noticed something I hadn't seen before. There was a bat phone hanging on the cave wall. Plain as day. Earlier, I had mistaken it for another bat. But, sure enough, there it was, a bat phone. The next question was who would I phone? And who might be monitoring my call? Questions, more questions. I felt trapped, but there were no negative thoughts lurking in my mind now. For some reason, I felt invigorated. I was on top of my game. And my meaning on this planet was becoming ever-more solid. My destiny was to help others, and what better way to do that than to serve as a private detective? The World-Ruler life was not for me. The requirements for the position were too demanding. As head of the New World Order, I would no longer be one LaFlam, but LaFlam plus Crusty, and, in addition, I would be Six plus Seven, equaling Thirteen, but, in the final equation, I'd be reduced to the lowest common denominator, which would be one-half of one big Hillbillary. This was too much to ask of any man, to become one flesh with another and having no hope of ever being divisible again. How odd life was. Here I was in my dark cave, the devious black light altering my reality, but my raison d'être had never been more together.

I grabbed the bat phone and pressed redial. Two rings, and a voice answered, "Dano, here." So my hunch had proved right.

"LaFlam here," I said. "Where are you?"

"Where are you? And who are you?"

"I'm Sissy's hired gun," I said. "And I'm here in a cave, under-cover, searching for you."

"Did Crusty put you up to this?"

That was encouraging. Sissy at least had been telling the truth. Crusty really had suckered Dano and now he was paying the price.

"No. I'm here representing Sissy in my latest case, The Case of Twelve."

"Who is this really?"

"LaFlam, Joe LaFlam, a private detective, hired by Sissy to find you, Jake Dano."

"What for?"

"Well, for Sissy, of course. She cares for you. You know that. And I would also like to find you to fulfill my obligation to Sissy, my client; plus, I'd like some help overthrowing Spelunkers Global and their scheme to rule the world."

"Forget it."

"What do you mean, forget it? If we don't stop them the world is done for."

"Let it go. There's nothing to do."

"I thought you anti-everythings were against this kind of Global oppression."

"I am, but if I do anything, my family will lose their fortune."

"Oh, they got you with that old one, too, eh? Well, if we don't do anything, we're going to be broke anyway. Since neither of us is going to be a number, we'll be herded with the masses and hooked up to the *Networks of Joy*, that is, if they don't kill us first. Why didn't you become a number?"

"Do you have any clue about what their idea of co-habitation is?"

"Yeah, sure, I know. They've already sized me up to fill that Maitraya suit. How did you get out? I didn't think you could get out."

"I'm not out. When I refused to be made into a composite, they forced me into doing pod duty. This way, my family survives."

"What did you do in real life?

"I was an investment banker."

"An investment banker? I thought you were an anti-everything type."

"Well, I am now, or at least I became one, after I dropped out of the whole corrupt system."

"Then why do you care about your family's fortune?"

"Blood's thicker than water from a fire hose."

"Do you think we can take them down?" I said.

"To be blunt, you don't inspire confidence."

"Oh, I get it. You mean there's something about my voice that's weak, don't you? I've often wondered about that. I don't like listening to myself on audio recordings either. I sound too nasal. Sometimes when I get cold viruses that go into my throat, I have this sharp bark that gets people's attention. Every time that happens, I hope that when the virus leaves my voice will stay the same, but that never happens. It always goes back to being nasal. I should have stood up for myself more when I was little, rather than cowing to authority figures."

"I can identify," Dano said. "I wasn't much of a banker, my father towering over me every minute of my life."

"I don't blame you for dropping out. My father wasn't there at all, but that's another story."

"No, there's no free ride in this life," he said. "Misery is the norm. Where are you, anyway?"

"I'm in a bat cave somewhere in the Spelunkers' compound."

"Are there lop-eared bunnies on your quilt?"

"Exactly," I said.

"So that's how you got me. Crusty phones me from there to taunt me about what was, and what might have been."

"How wicked," I said. "How could I ever have even considered...?"

"Have you told them yet you're not sold on androgyny?"

"No, I've been clever there. I haven't let on. And I've got at least three months before the big day."

"Don't count on it. You can't trust them. For that matter, they might be listening to us now. And if that's the case the jig is up."

"One other quick thing," I said, "what about Sissy?"

"She's a sweet kid. Too bad about her family. It makes you wonder doesn't it? How some kids grow up with everything, and, in this case, they're twins, and one is totally de-creative and the other is a precious earth goddess. Or, on the other hand, you can have two kids who grow up with virtually nothing, and one is destined for jail and the other for the White House. How does that happen?"

"I don't know. Those kinds of things are better left as mysteries. But, right now, let's hang up and wait, and see if they're onto us. If not, I'll call you back."

"Roger."

"I'm Joe," I said.

"I know."

"What's your number there?" I said.

"Six," Dano said.

"I'm Six."

"No, six is the Pods' extension."

"Oh, right, I see what you're saying, I dial six," I said.

"Roger," Dano said.

"I'm Joe."

"I know."

I hung up and waited. But what for? I wasn't sure. In the meantime, I decided to analyze every aspect of our current situation. Then I realized I was thinking for two now, Dano and me. Six said, *what about me?* But I turned a deaf ear. Yes, I felt a kindred spirit in Dano, even though he lived on the other side of the spiritual tracks. But the immediate question was, could I really get out of here if I wanted to? But did I want to, and was getting out of here the best course of action, or was it wiser to remain undercover? And if I did want to get out, could I find Dano first? And could we both get out if I did find him? And once out, if, in fact, we wanted to get out and could get out, what would we then do topside?

My rock slid open. Crusty burst through wearing a white silk shift, her hair and teeth shining like the sun. But now, to me, she was only glare. I decided to play along and see if she knew I'd found Dano.

"You look stunning," I said.

"Oh, thank you, Joe."

She called me Joe. We were safe for now.

"I like the dress," I said.

"It's a new Dior, Joe."

"You'll miss the fashion designers then, when they go into the vaporizer?"

"Oh, we'll keep a few for ourselves, Joe. Only the best for us. And we'll keep them under close scrutiny. We certainly won't let them escape to clothe the masses."

I decided to lighten up the conversation.

"So what do we do now, what's on the agenda, what's shakin', sister?"

"Please, Joe, I wish you wouldn't mention her name, even in jest."

So, the sibling rivalry was still intact, even though Crusty was a sure bet to win in the beat-the-twin game. She, who was slated to rule the world, remained jealous of sister Sissy. I decided to press in and see if she would play her evil hand.

"Sissy's not so bad. She has real feelings for that guy Dano."

"Sissy and Dano, Sissy and Dano, is that all you can talk about?"

"Sorry. Say, I'm wondering when I might get to see the pods."

"What for, Joe?"

"I'm anxious to see the place where we'll be made one, that's all."

"Oh, Joe, how romantic. Forgive me for being so petty. I realize you've been a private detective for a long time, and asking questions just goes with your territory. But we'll work that out of you. We'll be the perfect combination of questions and answers when we become one thing of stuff. Detective work will be eliminated, and we won't need any clues to go by. We'll live without a clue and without a care in the world. We will be able to think together, feel together, cry and laugh together, the perfect unit, and the future evolution of Star Stuff. We'll be the first one, Joe. We'll pioneer Stuff-oneness, and under our direction, more will follow, until the remaining Twelve have combined to make six. Next we will make from our own combined genes superior stuff for us to rule over, for we will always be the best stuff, Joe. Then all the inferior underlings will be obsolete and vaporizer bound. And then the rule of Onestuff will truly have begun, where all gender and identity confusion will cease, and we, you and I together Joe, we will be the progenitors, made of much better stuff, you and I, than those silly primitives, Adam and Eve. We will be the beginning of the Newest and Best Age ever, the Age of Onestuff."

"You really haven't seen *The Fly*, have you?"

"What's that supposed to mean, Joe?"

I winked.

"Oh, Joe, you get me every time. And just think, when we're finally together, we'll be able to wink as one."

I wondered who we were going to be winking at.

She continued, as if she read my mind, "We can wink at the stars, Joe, and they'll wink back, because we'll truly be the same as they are, and just as great, you'll see."

Yeah, sure, I would see, alright. She was as crazy as a bowler on steroids. And I knew if I crossed her, I'd end up guarding pods with Dano.

The light went on.

"I can't do it," I said.

"Can't do what?"

"Lose my identity. I have to be me."

"Joe...Joe...Joe, think what you're saying. You're throwing it all away, for what? So you can maintain your foolish quest for the elusive culprit, over and over again, till you die. What kind of life is that? And, besides, you know there won't be any need for private detectives in the age to come."

"I'll take my chances in this world with my genes intact, and my mind on straight and my meaning known."

"You're kidding, say you're kidding, Joe. You're destined for vaporization if you're not. And I would be saddened to see that happen."

"There are two kinds of people in this world," I said. "The takers and the givers. I'm going to be a giver. That's my meaning in life."

"You're a sucker, Joe. Everyone's a taker, at least everyone who's ever been given the opportunity to take."

"You're wrong, sister, and I use the term loosely. I'm going to stand for something in this world. And I'm going to expose every single taker I come across on this planet, and that especially includes Spelunkers Global."

"You've got one last chance, Joe. You either wink and say you're kidding or you are on temporary pod duty, until you're vaporized."

"And if I refuse, I suppose my family will lose their fortune."

"You've got it, Joe. You do have a detective's mind after all, don't you? Well, what's it to be? And don't lie to me either."

Yes, I could lie to her and buy time, or I could tell her the truth and do pod duty with Dano. Then we could engineer our escape, or plan their downfall, or something. We had to do something, Dano and I. But what? There again was the question. Dano said there was no escape, so the two of us together, a Christian private detective and an anti-everything, wouldn't add up to much. I knew then I had made a hasty decision. I had to change my mind again. I would lie for now and tell the truth later.

I winked and said, "You're all I'll ever need. I did want to be me, but I'm no good alone. I've never been good alone. I live in constant fear of rejection, and fear of sinking into depression. And only you hold the key to my ecstasy. I'll never be alone again, and rejection will no longer be an issue for me."

"Oh, Joe, you say the sweetest things. I knew you were just teasing me. Who wouldn't want to be Thirteen, and who wouldn't want to be the progenitor of a new line of ultimate Star Stuff? You are wise, Joe. Let's swear never to have this conversation again."

"Who to?"

"Oh, Joe, to each other, of course, silly."

"I swear to you," I said, crossing my fingers behind my back.

"And I swear to you, Joe," she said.

I'd crumbled again. Or had I actually been shrewd? What a question. Of course, I'd been shrewd not to tell the truth. But now what?

"Now what?" I said. "How do we prepare for the ultimate wedding?"

"Don't think of it as a wedding, Joe. Think of it as the pinnacle of evolution, when we join the stars as one."

I'd had enough of this. She was always correcting me. I'd say tamaydah, and she'd say tamahtah. I wanted again to call the whole thing off. Why couldn't she see that together we would rip our self apart? Ah, but who could blame her? She grew up underground, with Papa as her dad, and good Sissy as her sister. She enjoyed being closed in, and she, no doubt craved security, and what better security could there be in her Godless universe than to be inextricably spliced with another piece of star dirt. She would never sleep alone again, or do anything alone again. I would be there in our side.

The rock slid open again, and there stood Papa. He was smiling.

"Are you lovebirds going to invite me in?" Papa said.

"Sure, come on in," I said. "Why not? It's a free country."

"Not for long," Papa said. Papa then broke into a laugh, and Crusty laughed, too.

I grinned and winked at Crusty. The cave was alight with teeth. Some days undercover work was hard.

Crusty said, "Joe is indeed our hope for the future, Papa."

"And you, daughter, don't forget about you. I'm such a proud Papa."

To show how proud Papa was, he puffed up his chest and bellowed, "Long live Maitraya." He then bowed to us both and turning, toddled back out the door.

"He's a darling," Crusty said to me and then followed him out.

I saw no reason to agree.

"Now what?" I yelled after her.

"See you at lunch," she called back. "Chuckles will come for you."

I slid my rock shut. Eating seemed to be their main priority around here. But now what? What about Alfred and Abner? Was contacting them a good idea? The bat phone was still hanging there. Why not just dial my office? Papa and Crusty seemed to trust me; they hadn't tapped my call to Dano, unless they were good actors. But were the phone lines connected to the world above ground? And if they were, what would Alfred and Abner be able to do for me? Still, there was strength in numbers. And if we succeeded in springing Dano, then there would be four of us. And, besides,

Alfred knew how these vermin ticked. I hadn't wanted to put my partners at risk, but I could see no other option now. But could they get in, or we get out? Time would tell. Although, it was easy to lose your sense of time underground. There was no sun or moon to go by. Time was eternal down here. What a place to live, suited only for bugs and moles and dead bodies, situated as it was, one floor above hell.

I reached for the phone and dialed.

"Bell, Booker, and LaFlam," Alfred said.

"It's me. Where's Pen, on a break?"

"Yes, she's out. I wondered when you would get around to calling."

"I've been busy, and I don't have much time right now, although it's hard to tell down here."

"You've been underground too long, by the sound of it."

"I need help."

"Well, we've known that for a while."

"No, I mean, it's worse than I thought. I need you and Abner to help me spring Dano. I've found him."

"Abner's gone."

"What?"

"He left, yesterday. He said that since you were backsliding, why shouldn't he?"

"Abner's gone?" I said.

"Yes, Abner's gone."

My stomach turned. "I don't want to be on this line too long. I'll call you back, and then I'll tell you where I am."

"I know where you are."

"You do?"

"There's a bug in your fedora."

"I gotta go. I'll call you back."

"When?"

I hung up. I was a failure. That fact hit me long and hard. I'd let Abner down in my quest to find meaning in my life, when all along one of my main meanings was to help Abner and, of course, Alfred, and anyone else who might be looking to be mentored by a mature Christian detective. But in my own defense, I did believe at the time my duty was to help Sissy. Or did I? Maybe I just wanted to be a hero, the one who brought Spelunkers Global down. But maybe my destiny wasn't to bring Spelunkers Global down. Maybe my destiny was to escape and forget I ever heard of anyone named Dano, or Sissy, or Spelunkers Global for that matter. Abner needed me now. I had to find him, or die trying. Maybe a life in my parents' hotel business was my real future. No, that line of thinking was all wrong, not to mention I'd fallen again into the quagmire of negative thoughts. Was there no way out? Papa promised we'd lose our family fortune if I didn't cooperate. So that made my family's future my responsibility. They needed me to persevere. The only way through was through. There was no going back, or around, or over, and certainly there was no going under. The red light flashed on the silent bat phone. No, there was nothing I could do about Abner right now.

"Yeah?" I said, into a bat ear.

"Why don't I just come and get you?" Alfred said.

"You can't do that. They'll kill you."

"Have you seen any armed guards? Any guns?"

"Uh, no."

"What's keeping you there, then?"

"Well, they're going to ruin the family business, not to mention I'm on my mission to expose them for the evil megalomaniacs they are."

"What laws have they broken?"

"They've got Dano, and they plan to take over the world, isn't that enough?"

"Are you sure they're Spelunkers?"

"Of course they're Spelunkers. They've got the caves and the bats and the pods and the evil schemes and everything."

"I have my doubts," Alfred said.

"What do you mean?"

"Somebody just came in. He wants to talk to you."

"Who?"

"Ya think yer a real private eye, now don't ya?" Abner said.

"Abner, boy am I happy to hear you're back," I said.

"Don't get mushy. Anyway, I didn't go very far. I started to; I even had the bottle up to my lips. But then I realized my faith didn't count on you. And then I got mad. Why should I go on sufferin' just because my mentor's a backslider?"

"Wait a minute, Abner, I'm not backsliding."

"What do ya call it then?"

"I'm just doing my job. The job I've been hired to do."

"You been lyin' and cheatin', haven't ya?"

My rock slid open, and I hung up on Abner's accusation.

"Lunch is served," Chuckles said, eyeing me and the phone.

"I'm with you," I said.

"You think you're somebody, don't you," Chuckles said, "just because you're a full-blown number now?"

Chuckles turned, and I followed him out. Every time I saw Chuckles now he was more jealous of me. Still, I wondered if I might turn him against Papa and Crusty.

"Do you like life around here?" I said, following Chuckles down the bat hall.

"Is that a threat?"

"No, what I mean is, do you see yourself serving in this place forever?"

"Have you got any better ideas?"

I left it at that, but I concluded from his reply that he was open to other possibilities. An uprising might be possible. I had to find Dano and see if there were any others who might want to make a break for it.

"In here," Chuckles said.

There they were, Papa and Crusty, seated at their flat rock table in their cozy cave. A plate of sandwiches, cut in squares with the crusts removed, occupied Papa's attention. Crusty's broad smile seemed to say, *I love you.*

"Sit, Joe, sit," she said.

Would she want me to roll over next?

Papa, a sandwich square in each hand, said, "Haba sandwich."

"And try this Bat Beer, Joe," Crusty said, "a specialty of the cave."

Bat Beer? I wondered what they made it from.

"What's it made from?" I said.

"You don't want to know," Papa said.

I sat down, and she poured me a large tankard full of the yellow stuff. What did I have to lose? I wasn't a drinker, but what was a little Bat Beer among friends? There was nothing like a cold brew on a hot day. That's what they always said, those macho guys who slugged it down like it didn't taste like yellow swill. Anybody with a brain knew that anything cold and wet tasted good on a hot day. Although, in Bible times, they did drink wine. But, I would never want to make a brother or sister stumble by drinking in front of them. What would Abner think if he saw me sitting here, eating liver paté sandwiches and drinking Bat Beer? But Abner wasn't here, so I was free to do as my conscience dictated. And there was no chance I was going to cause Papa and Crusty to stumble. They'd fallen a long time ago. Then again, I had to be a good witness. But Papa and Crusty were ignorant of the debate over whether Christians should drink or not. So, in this instance, to drink or not to drink had nothing to do with being a good witness. On the other hand, I didn't want to use alcohol as a crutch to give me courage. I was brave enough without it. I sniffed. The brew smelled like taco shells and bat caves. I pinched my nose from the inside and took a swallow. It went down hard. Sensing the need to maintain a good image, I suppressed a gag, wiped my mouth with the back of my hand, shook my head in appreciation, and then stifled a belch.

"That's good Bat," I said and grabbed a deviled egg to erase the taste.

"I knew you'd like it, Joe," Crusty said.

"I'm not a drinker, but I can appreciate the finer things."

"You're so sweet, Joe," Crusty said.

Papa held off on his next sandwich long enough to say, "How did you like our plan?"

"Superb, I couldn't have created a better one."

"Oh, sure you could have, Joe," Crusty said.

"But something's puzzled me for a few years now," I said.

"Maybe we can help," Papa said, "you're one of the Twelve now."

"Well, you know those contrails that jets sometimes make across the sky over major cities? Some say they're really chemtrails. They're not like normal contrails that disappear after a few minutes. These trails kind of hang up there and spread out, and they usually run in parallel lines, like they're plowing a field up there, and sometimes they're in X-patterns, or crosshatched like tic-tac-toe. And there are these theories that dark forces are testing aerosols on the environment and on the people. Some say they're trying to block out the sun's rays to prevent global warming. Others say the chemtrails are causing diseases, and some say they are an attempt to control the weather, and others even say they're some kind of way to control populations by using mind-altering chemicals to bring the nations into submission. I didn't see anything about that in your take-over-the-world presentation, and I just wonder what those trails really are."

Papa looked at Crusty, shook his head, and said, "It's the stuff that comes out of the back of jet engines."

Crusty nodded her head. So, mystery solved. I decided to push my luck. Although, of course, as everyone knew by now, I didn't believe in luck.

"Well, what about that secret group, the Gardenbergers, the ones who are supposed to be making all the major decisions in the world, supported by all the rich banking families. Who are they anyway?"

Papa said, "Minor players in the game."

"Minor players?" I said.

Crusty and Papa nodded.

"Well, then what about Henry Kissinger?"

"Isn't that the professor?" Papa said to Crusty.

"Yes, Papa, you know the one, he has that deep voice that vibrates like a bass fiddle. A lot of fun at a party."

"Oh, right," Papa said. It's really too bad he's so bright. Too bright for his own good."

So, Dr. Kissinger was headed for the vaporizer. Would there be no justice left on this planet earth?

"Then what about the Council on Foreign Relations, and the Tri-lateral Commission and the World Bank?"

"Smoke screens," Papa said.

I decided to ask the big one. "Okay, then what about the Illuminati?"

Crusty answered this one, "Just a lot of hocus-pocus. They don't exist. Don't you see, Joe? We're the future, and the future is now."

I was beginning to feel uneasy. How did the Spelunkers manage to get control? They seemed too inept to rule the world, not to mention the fact they chose me as their hope for the future. Not that there was anything wrong with me. I was a good choice really. No more negative thoughts for me. But they must have worked out some ingenious method of control to get all the power-brokers of the world to join and obey them. And what kind of method was that? The only conclusion to be drawn was that they were pure evil. Only pure evil was able to control the world system, which meant Papa and Crusty were not the average father and daughter they pretended to be. There was something deeper going on. As usual, it was hard to tell who was doing what in the game evil played. And sometimes evil came in pretty packages and was hard to pin down. Surface evil was easy to see, but down-deep evil was a horse of a different color. It was obvious by the state of things that real evil had been running the world for some time. And I also understood now that real evil wasn't that easy to catch, so how was I going to bust evil, and what judge on earth was going to convict it?

"Why are you staring far away like that, Joe?" Crusty said.

I swallowed another shot of bat juice and considered my answer.

"Must be the Bat Beer," I said, grabbing for another deviled egg.

"Oh, it's just slightly hallucinogenic," Crusty said.

So that explained my recent insight into evil. It took one to know one. A little evil down the hatch, and my thoughts had turned to evil, although in this case, I had only plumbed the depths of evil, rather than becoming it.

"Evil's a funny thing," I said.

"Evil, Joe?" Crusty said. "What do you mean, evil?"

Papa looked up from his asparagus sandwich, his face quizzical. Crusty exchanged glances with Papa and then continued, "Let's get this straight, Joe, once and for all. Evil is a human construct created to explain certain behaviors. Behaviors just are. We are Star Stuff behaving, that's all. There is no reason to believe in anything, good or bad. Existence is. We exist and we continue to exist until we don't, and then we exist in another form, which is just other stuff. Got it?"

"It must have been the beer again," I said with a wink.

"Oh, of course it was, Joe, I knew it all along."

Papa nodded and smiled. All was right again with the under-world. So, I'd come face-to-face with evil. Well, they weren't going to get me, and they weren't going to get the millions of others on this planet who knew they weren't just stuff. I knew how this age ended, and while it wasn't going to look very pretty for a while, in the end these purveyors of the New Age of Onestuff would be toast.

"What's the timetable?" I said.

Papa said, "In a few months. The nuclear devices first. Strategically placed. Soften up the ground. A biological weapon here and there, nothing major, a plague or two, an incurable flu. Get the masses eager for someone to save them. Then, boom, here we are. Larger than life to save the day. Case closed, eh, LaFlam? Get it? Case closed?"

Papa's joy boomed, debris flying from his face's orifices, and then he sputtered to a halt. I forced a smile for Crusty.

"So, Joe, you see? It's all settled," she said.

"Yeah, it's in the bag," I said.

I decided to spring the big question.

"Do you think I'll be able to go back and tie up some loose ends, you know, with my business and my family?"

"Sure, Joe, we trust you, don't we Papa?"

Papa slugged back his tankard of Bat Beer, slammed the empty on the rock table, and issued an oath.

"That means 'yes'," Crusty said.

I was relieved. They were going to let me out of here. I was going to be able to sit down with Alfred and Abner and work out a way to foil their wicked scheme. And I would see Sissy again, lovely Sissy with the long sharp nose. I looked at Crusty's nose. It was evil. Not in-your-face evil, but evil nonetheless. On the other hand, Sissy's nose was attached to goodness. She was worth fighting for. But my feelings for Sissy had to finish second to my main meaning in this life, and that was to help others by remaining true to the private detective's code of honor. At my own future's expense, I was bound to do nothing less than rescue her Jake.

"I'll be coming with you, Joe," Crusty said. "And Chuckles is coming, too. It'll be fun tying up your loose ends."

I didn't like the sound of that. I could hear the lilt of evil in Crusty now. Funny how you could see a person a certain way one day, and the next day that person was someone else, even though they walked and talked and carried on the same. In an instant, their souls were bare, and you knew what made them tick, or, at least, I'd heard that some people were able to do that. I wasn't that intuitive.

But this time I'd pierced Crusty and Papa's veil. My ability to see evil had deepened, and for the benefit of my future cases, I hoped this new discernment would endure, even though people's interiors were often unlovely to look at. And then I had a further insight. I envisioned who they might have been had they not fallen into the underworld's foul soup. He might have been a senator or head of the UN, and she might have been a journalist or an actress. She would have made a great actress, except for the nose. But they would be none of those now. It was too late for them. Evil had them, and they didn't even know it. They had eliminated the concept from their world. There was no doubt about it, evil could spoil a life. I then reflected on the course of world history and on my own history, and I could see that many nations and many relationships had been ruined by evil. Yes, evil took, and kept on taking.

"There you go, staring off in the distance again, Joe," Crusty said.

"Powerful Bat Beer," I said and tossed her another wink.

CHAPTER TWENTY-THREE

My office was cool, the way an air-conditioned office could be cool during a pre-summer heat-wave in the Pacific Northwest. Outside, far below, the denizens of the cleared rain forest fretted their way through the baking city streets. I relished being here at the top, in perfect position to help others less fortunate. My plan was solid and established now. I would wed *noblesse oblige* and detective work to serve the masses, and no Spelunker scum was going to bring me down, not when I was on top of my game, knowing as I did now, who I was and what my purpose was. The Spelunkers were the ones who were going to be brought down, although in a way they were already down, and, in fact, I was going to go down to bring them up to bring them down. Or if I had to bring them down when they were on their way up, that's what I would do. Or something like that.

My office was not only cool on this particular sweltering day in late spring; it was silent, the way a penthouse detective's office could be stone-cold silent when the detectives and the evil villains squared off face-to-face. We sat there, Alfred, Abner, Crusty, Chuckles and I, all cooperating to help wind up my affairs. That's what it looked like we were doing, but, in fact, I was only pretending to wind up my affairs and say goodbye, while Alfred was doing a poor job of not showing contempt for Crusty and Chuckles. Crusty and Chuckles were trying not to appear suspicious of us, and Abner was doing a poor job of pretending not to be bored. I'd just finished explaining to Alfred and Abner that we were in transition, that nothing stayed the same, that life fluxed. They had received my insights well, knowing that I was stalling, and knowing that I was searching for an opportunity to talk to them alone, free from the spying eyes of Crusty and Chuckles. Abner cracked our brief, embarrassed silence.

"So," Abner said, "what now? Are we all goin' to just sit here fer the rest of the day?"

Alfred frowned at Abner, and Abner turned to Chuckles and grimaced. Chuckles stared back, a blank look on his face.

I said to Alfred and Abner, "So, as you see, I'm going to be leaving the detective business. It's not easy for me, but I'm being called to a higher purpose."

"Backslider," Abner said.

"And I'm leaving the business to you both. The lease is paid up for another year, as is Pen's salary. I talked to her, and she's willing to stay on for that long at least. That should give you time to become more well known and work up a client list."

"What makes ya think I want to be a private eye?" Abner said. "I was only joinin' cause I thought you were goin' to raise me up in the faith like you promised."

I couldn't understand why Abner was making the transaction difficult, when he knew I was putting on an act for Crusty and Chuckles. That's assuming Alfred had informed Abner of the facts of our current situation. Or maybe Abner thought making life difficult for me was his part in the act. Who knew?

"We'll take the business," Alfred said, "and we wish you the best in all your future endeavors."

"Yeah, break a leg," Abner said.

"Well," I said, "I guess that wraps things up. See you in church tomorrow."

"Yer comin' to church?" Abner said. "What for?"

"Leave him alone," Alfred said.

"Church?" Crusty said. She glanced over at Chuckles who furrowed his scar.

"Yeah," I said. "I want to say goodbye to Pastor Bernard and the congregation."

"Joe," Crusty said, "we won't give them any details, will we?"

"No, but I need to bid a final farewell to them all, to bring closure to LaFlam."

"I understand, Joe," Crusty said. "You are wise. I'm glad you do see the need to start fresh. We wouldn't want any of LaFlam's residue left in us. We'd only have to clean it up after our union."

"LaFlam residue?" Abner said. "What's LaFlam residue? You ain't plannin' to fly off to join some spaceship, are ya?"

Abner then sneered at Crusty and added, "Sure, I knew it. I told ya before. Ya can't trust nobody with yellow eyes. They's aliens, every one of 'em."

"We're Star Stuff," Crusty said. "You would do well to remember that."

"Ya threatenin' me?" Abner said. "Ya can't scare me so easy. I had the DTS so bad back in '93, I thought I was bein' interviewed naked on the Oprah show. After somethin' like that, there's not much more ya can do to a guy."

"Abner," Alfred said, "why don't we let Joe do what he has to do?"

"Sure, see ya in church," Abner said.

"We'll all have a lovely time," Crusty said. "I haven't been to one in years."

"You're coming to church?" I said.

"And Chuckles, too, Joe," she said. "Don't forget Chuckles."

So, there was no shaking loose from them. They were hanging on to me like a bat caught in big hair. But what would Crusty and Chuckles do in church? Would they be able to sit there, would the evil in Crusty be able to go to church and feel comfortable? Then again, maybe I was being too narrow-minded; maybe there was still a chance for both of them. They might hear the message tomorrow and take it to heart. It was never too late to be saved, was it?

I diverted their attention by pressing the button on the intercom, and with the other hand I pretended to scratch my leg, as I removed my spare cell phone from my lower desk drawer.

"Okay, Pen, that's all for today," I said.

"Are you still my boss?" Pen said.

"I see. Well, you can consider this my last instruction to you," I said.

"Fair enough," Pen said. "I would like to say I'll miss you."

"I can't hardly wait for church tomorrow," Abner said. "It'll be a service to remember."

Now that I had the cell phone in my pocket, all I needed was the opportunity to use it. I had to talk to Alfred about our plan, and then I had to assure Sissy that her man Dano was going to be okay.

Alfred said, "Where are you staying tonight?"

"I'm going to see if Aunt Margaret will put us up for the night. That'll give me an opportunity for a visit."

"We'll love that, Joe," Crusty said, "won't we, Chuckles?"

Chuckles managed a nod but showed no emotion. Abner and Alfred, at the mention of Aunt Margaret, had perked up.

"How about if I come over later for a little visit?" Abner said.

"If you're going over, then there will be two of us going," Alfred said.

"Oh, good, we'll have a party, Joe," Crusty said.

"Ya got that right, sister," Abner said.

CHAPTER TWENTY-FOUR

What a joy it was to see Aunt Margaret. It seemed like ages had passed since I'd last seen her. For her it was an enchanted night. Memories of her flower-childhood were in full bloom. She was of necessity older now, a demand the hourglass puts on us all, the sands of time sifting us, as we journeyed to our final heartbeat. But tonight she was forever young, for she had two suitors wooing her, and reminding her of the flourishing vigor of her '60s prime. But of course, the memory of what was, in truth, her youthful folly, had not escaped her mind either, for Aunt Margaret was not a foolish, selfish Boomer. She had learned from the past, unlike so many others who had cut and pasted their '60s past into their Google search for more. Yes, Aunt Margaret was content with her world and with us, her companions, this humid evening, and, true to her generous nature, she was anxious for our motley crew to have ourselves a time to remember.

She had received us well, opening her home to Crusty and Chuckles with the slightest of objections. Where she would put us all was her only concern, though we knew by her buoyant tone that she would indeed find a place for us. Alfred and Abner arrived in typical courting fashion, like bickering schoolboys, hair slicked back with spit, eager to get on with the hunt. And I, and Chuckles, well we had been into the Bat Beer again, I having purloined a few bottles for our travels. The living room was warm but tolerable. I suspected, though, that the humidity would begin to wear, as our mortal coils, confined to the small room, heated up.

"You're in pharmaceuticals research, then Crusty?"Aunt Margaret said, sipping her fruit juice and ginger ale, a favorite punch she'd mixed for the occasion.

"No, DNA."

"DNA, well, dear me, DNA," Aunt Margaret said. "What does that stand for? I've heard it so often, of course, but never stopped to consider what it meant. Then again, I've never had a DNA expert to talk to before."

"Deoxyribonucleic acid," Crusty said.

"Acid? How, je ne sais quoi."

Alfred and Abner were on the edge of their seats, focusing on Aunt Margaret, each nestling his punch.

"Crusty's at the head of her field," I said.

"You can really pick them, John," Aunt Margaret said.

"John?" Crusty said.

More than amused, Chuckles grinned at the revelation.

"Yeah," I said, "it's the name I was born with."

"John LaFlam?" Crusty said.

"Uh, no, John Doe actually."

"Doe? Oh, Joe! Smith and Doe together," Crusty said, elated. "That's perfect."

I was amazed at Crusty's exuberance, though I shouldn't have been. Tonight evil was putting her best, pretty face forward, though it really wasn't that pretty. But on the other hand, the same face looked good on Sissy. It only proved that it was the insides that counted. When the devil was in control, your outward appearance was bound to suffer, maybe not immediately, maybe not in a few years, maybe not for decades, but time would have its way, but then again, after decades you would be way older anyway and aging fast, which would make it difficult for you to know if your failing image was natural aging or the devil's dirty work. I examined my most recent thoughts and vowed never to touch the Bat Beer again.

I said, "I thought you already knew my real name, and when I was born, and the alignment of the stars."

"Oh, I suppose we did," Crusty said, "but I don't do that kind of research. They only told me you were the one."

"We Christians don't believe in astrology," Aunt Margaret said.

"It's about Star Stuff," Crusty said, "not about horoscopes."

"Ya, and I'm an Asparagus," Abner said.

Chuckles chuckled, having found something funny in Abner's remark, and then, for the second time since I'd met him, his face doubled up with laughter. I began to wonder again if Chuckles might be redeemable, or was his genial outburst only a side effect of the Bat Beer?

"Oh, we're having such a lovely time," Aunt Margaret said, rolling her punch glass in her hands, the condensation perceptible, as it moistened and cooled her fingers. Alfred and Abner were captivated. This kind of behavior never looked good on old people, but why be critical? They had a right to a life, too.

Aunt Margaret continued, "And what fabulous news. You and Crusty tying the knot."

"The old ball and chain," Abner said for effect.

"When's the date?" Aunt Margaret said.

"In a few months," I said. "We haven't set the exact date."

"Oh, Joe," Crusty said, "we'll be bound forever soon."

Crusty's act was wearing me down, and the Bat Beer was spinning the room.

"Are you okay?" Alfred said.

"I think he's drunk," Abner said. "Fine thing, my spiritual mentor lost in the sauce."

Chuckles hiccupped for everybody.

"Ya both been in the sauce, haven't ya?" Abner said.

"I'm not drunk, Abner," I said. "It's just that the heat's getting to me in here."

"Backslider."

"Oh, Abner, be nice," Aunt Margaret said. "You know that John is a fine young man."

"He ain't that young," Abner said. "He shoulda been married years ago, and now look what it's come to."

Abner rolled his eyes in Crusty's direction.

"You don't have to like me," Crusty said, feigning hurt feelings.

"NO, NO," everyone but Abner said, "WE ALL LIKE YOU."

It seemed nobody, except Abner, wanted to hurt evil's feelings and spoil the evening.

"You remember, dear," Aunt Margaret said to Crusty, "don't let others define you, especially men."

Little did Aunt Margaret know that evil Crusty was planning to eliminate men, and women too, for that matter. Aunt Margaret wasn't tuned into this present darkness of our time. She lived in her own time, a time she had been born into, just as we all were. Billions of Homo sapiens, over the millennia, had been born into their own time here on good old terra firma. We all had our time to be; we weren't allowed to live in another generation's time, neither the one before us, nor the one after us. And if we tried to, our peers would judge us as unstable, like one of the brothers rapping *The Sound of Music* on a hillside in the Alps.

Chuckles said, "Yes, don't worry, Ms. Smith, you're performing well."

Crusty dropped her affected air of being consoled to raise an eyebrow at Chuckles, who had, under the influence, broken master-servant protocol. I sensed rebellion growing in Chuckles, and that, I hoped, would prove useful in our future bust of evil.

A flash of light lit up the front window. We waited. The rumble grew and then exploded, shaking our little party.

"Oooh," Aunt Margaret said, "I love the cleansing of the air."

"Ya always loved a good storm," Abner said.

Butting in on Abner, Alfred said, "So, Margaret, how's your new craft store coming?"

"Oh, you're in crafts," Crusty said. "How…interesting."

"Sales are improving steadily," Aunt Margaret said. "It was so good of John to set me up in the business." Aunt Margaret then locked onto Crusty's eyes and added confidentially, "He does have a good heart. Don't you worry, dear."

Aunt Margaret really knew how to encourage me, recommending me the way she did to one of the top-dogs of the anti-Christ system. But then again, was Crusty a part of that corrupt system? I was beginning to have my doubts. The anti-Christ was by all accounts a spiritual kind of being, but Crusty's gig was impersonal Star Stuff. If she was in truth part of that system, she wasn't being too scriptural about it.

"I'm not worried, Aunt Margaret," Crusty said. "Joe and I, well, we were made for each other."

"Oh, splendid," Aunt Margaret said, "John has finally met his match."

White light flashed at the window again, and then the thunder and my stomach both rumbled together. The Bat Beer had taken its toll. I wondered if that last bottle we drank had been brewed from a batch of rabid bats.

"Yeah, they're a pair," Abner said.

Aunt Margaret, satisfied with her interview of the happy couple, and excited by the electricity in the air, said, "Why don't we all dance?"

Alfred looked at Aunt Margaret and then at Abner, who looked at Aunt Margaret and then jumped from his chair to find the right CD.

Aunt Margaret said, "Play *Summertime*, Abner, I love *Summertime*."

Abner found the CD and slid the disc in. He next made his way straight to Aunt Margaret's chair, but Alfred outmaneuvered him.

"Shall we?" Alfred said.

Abner plunked himself down in his chair, mumbling, "Cheater," under his breath.

"Ooh, let's, Joe," Crusty said.

So it had come to this. I had to dance with the devil.

Aunt Margaret slow danced with Alfred and crooned along, "Ooh, summertime, and the livin' is easy, the fish are jumpin', and the cotton is high..."

Crusty snuggled into me, and I lost my resolve for a few seconds. I recovered and remembered who she really was. She wasn't the woman of my dreams. And she certainly wasn't the future Mrs. LaFlam. No, she was the purveyor of all that was evil on this planet, not just an armful of supple flesh to dance with on this hot, spring evening. And would I never marry?

I heard Chuckles say to Abner above the music, "I thought you devoted Christian types didn't believe in dancing."

"We're Charismatics now," Abner said.

Chuckles looked puzzled, but kept his good humor. "What's a Charismatic?" he said.

"I'm not altogether sure yet," Abner said, "but so far I know we're the kind of Christians that likes the gifts."

"Oh, is that so?" Chuckles said. "What gifts?"

"We all got gifts," Abner said. "Some use 'em, some don't, but they say we're all brothers and sisters under the skin."

Chuckles started to ask Abner more about the faith, but Abner's focus had shifted. He saw his opportunity and jumped up, aiming to cut in on Alfred, which he did, Aunt Margaret relishing the attention and Alfred sulking back to his chair. For my part in the dance, I was weary of the battle between surfaces and essences. I had to stop. I let go of her.

"Oh, Joe, we just started," Crusty whined.

"Sorry, I've got two left feet tonight."

"No you don't, you only stepped on me twice."

"Sorry. And it's getting late, too."

"Oh, Joe, let's don't end the party yet."

Summertime was winding down, and so was Aunt Margaret. She disengaged from Abner and began to fan herself with her hand.

Overcome by the coalescence of her memories and her present reality, she flopped into her chair.

"Ooh, I could have danced all night," she said, and then laughed at her obscure allusion to *My Fair Lady*.

Alfred, unhappy the dancing might have ended for the evening, scowled at Abner.

"That was fun," Aunt Margaret added. "Maybe we can dance more later?" Then, turning her attention to Crusty, she said, "And your family, what's your family like, Crusty?"

"Oh, my Papa is a gem, a wonderful gem, a perfect specimen of Star Stuff, and my mom—"

"What about her sister?" Abner said. "Ask her about her sister, Sissy."

Crusty's face cracked, her ebullient smile's bubbles bursting in air. Below her blonde helmet, darkness encompassed her yellow eyes.

"Let's don't talk about her," Crusty spat.

At the sight of Crusty's venom, Aunt Margaret's head was taken aback, a swirl of punch slopping over the rim of her glass. Alfred and Abner watched the silly drop fall on her Mama Cass flowered sack. Aunt Margaret frowned. The night had been ruined, and we all knew it. Alfred cast a black look Abner's way.

"Well," I said. "We've got a big day tomorrow, I guess it's time—"

"What do ya mean?" Abner said. "Tomorrow's no bigger than any other day. We all got time to hear about her sister Sissy, ain't we?"

I saw that Abner wasn't to be dissuaded from his desire to stay and spend more time with Aunt Margaret.

"Please, Joe," Crusty said. "Make him stop. I don't want to cause a scene."

Aunt Margaret canvassed us for more information, "Is her sister not nice?" she said.

"Nice? She's a vixen," Crusty barked.

"Take's one to know one," Abner said.

"That's going too far," Alfred said to Abner.

"Really, Abner," Aunt Margaret said. "And you, John, aren't you going to defend your bride?"

"She can hold her own," I said.

Chuckles began to laugh, the Bat Beer no doubt encouraging him.

Alfred said, "Maybe it would be better if we all got a good night's sleep."

We all, including Abner, nodded our heads. I had, just a moment ago, tried to suggest that same thing. But nobody had listened to me. They'd listened to Alfred but not me. That was typical. Nobody ever listened to me, even when my decisions were right. I had doubted my leadership abilities for years. Oh, oh, there it was again, I had to stop. I was only feeling sorry for myself. Worse still, my mind's rapid descent from the Bat Beer high had plopped me into a vat of negative confessions. Would I never get out?

Aunt Margaret showed Abner and Alfred to the door, where Abner punctuated his leaving by gushing, "Till we meet again," and kissed Aunt Margaret's hand, as lightning flashed and thunder rumbled on cue.

Alfred said to Abner, "Smooth, really smooth." And to Aunt Margaret, he said, "Will we see you in church tomorrow?"

"Oh, Alfred," she said, cheerful again, "I wouldn't miss it for the world."

Alfred and Abner departed, and we were now faced with the details of spending the night. Aunt Margaret began to dish out some good-natured teasing by saying Crusty and I certainly wouldn't be staying together in my room, at least not until we had tied the knot. She decided, however, that my room would be perfect for Crusty, and, as for us, Chuckles and me, we were invited to sleep on cots in her crafts workshop above the garage.

"It'll do," she said. "And while we're on the subject, where are you and Crusty going to live after you're married?"

I was at a loss on this one, but my future soul mate came to the rescue. "My family has arranged for a cozy little condo at an undisclosed location."

"Ooh, how intimate," Aunt Margaret said.

Aunt Margaret didn't know, of course, just how intimate it would be. But then how could anyone possibly know the depths of the Spelunkers' diabolical mating. No, it couldn't be known.

Crusty said, "What a joy to sleep alone in the boyhood room of my future same flesh, my future same everything."

"Well," Aunt Margaret said, "you have certainly taken your Biblical instruction to heart."

"That's Biblical?" Crusty said.

"Never mind," I said, pecking Aunt Margaret's cheek and shaking Crusty's hand goodnight.

"Not very passionate," Aunt Margaret said, referring to my shaking of Crusty's hand. "I would have expected, considering the length of time it's taken you to...."

"Okay, Chuckles, are you ready to hit the hay?" I said.

"Never mind, dear," Aunt Margaret said to Crusty, "he's a gentle young man, and he'll come around eventually."

"No need," Crusty said, "there's more to life than just that."

"You young people," Aunt Margaret said. "You are a strange bunch. But then again the next generation is always like that, different from the previous one. I remember in the '60s, our parents didn't understand us, either, and...."

"Fine, goodnight," I said.

Chuckles and I left them there to discuss generational differences and headed with our overnight bags to the loft above the garage.

Our quarters were Spartan. Two cots, two sleeping bags, two cushions stuffed into pillow cases. I let Chuckles pick, and he took the one under the window. We decided to sleep in our clothes and change in the house in the morning.

"I got some Bat," Chuckles said.

"Not for me," I said. "I'm swearing off, and you might want to remember there's no bathroom out here either."

This piece of intelligence didn't seem to bother Chuckles. He found his stash, sat on his cot, and unscrewed the cap from a bottle. He swigged and belched. Taco-chips and bat-cave odor clung to the air.

"How can you drink more of that stuff?" I said, nestling into my sleeping bag.

"It's company," Chuckles said.

"So, why do you stay with them?" I said, again looking for chinks in his armor. "Have they got something on you, too?"

"Why so nosy? And what are you up to? I'm not a traitor if that's what you're getting at."

"Don't worry, I'm one of them now, remember? We're all *us* now."

Chuckles took my word for it and lightened up a little.

"The pay's good, free room and board and Bat Beer. What more could you ask for?"

"A room above ground," I said.

"We'll all be up soon, and as you already know, we'll have the best. Mine won't be as good as yours, but I'm not complaining."

I was disappointed that Chuckles was content with his lot in life. I was hoping he would be more complex.

"Any ambitions?" I said.

"No, I lost my ambition when I was rejected as a number. I'm relieved in a way. No responsibility. There's nothing wrong with being head servant to the World Rulers." He took a long pull on his Bat Beer and added, "No. Not too shabby."

"No, Chuckles, there's nothing wrong with having a servant's heart."

"Is that something Christian?"

"What?"

"What you just said about having a servant's heart?"

"Yeah, it's Christian," I said. "Serving others is what it's all about. And forgiveness."

"You're not going to be much of a World Ruler with that attitude," he said.

"What do you think you might have done in life, Chuckles? You know, what would your meaning in life have been, if you hadn't signed on as a servant to the World Rulers?"

"Meaning?" he said. "That's pretty deep, isn't it?" I could see that the Bat Beer was taking the remaining edge off Chuckles. "I don't know," he said, staring at the floor. "I did have an interest in theater, when I was in college. You know, acting. I was drawn to the production end and directing, too. But it takes plenty of brains and skill and talent to do that, and I would probably have failed. Probably it all worked out for the best this way."

"Hey, that's a negative attitude," I said. "You need to make positive confessions to succeed in life."

"Confessions? You're not Catholic, are you? Or are Charismatics Catholic?"

"Some of them, but I'm an Evangelical, an evangelical Charismatic, or, let's see, how can I explain?"

"You people are weird."

"Forget the Church and theology and all that right now. I'm just trying to encourage you. Your dreams might come true yet."

"Are you kidding me? But come to think of it, I do help with some of the hologram productions. And I'm getting better at it, but I'll never be able to learn it all."

"You can do it, Chuckles. What's stopping you? That's what the American Dream is all about."

"American Dream? The American Dream will soon be waking up, and you better not say any more. Or I'll have to report you to Ms. Smith."

"Come on, Chuckles, you were made for better things than this. This is America, and anyone can grow up to be anything they want to be. All you need is enough gumption to take a run at life, set your goals, dream your big dreams, be daring. Set your vision on conquering any mountain that's set before you. You don't have to settle for playing second-fiddle, when you were born to be a conductor. Wave your baton, Chuckles, wave it for all to see."

Chuckles, entranced, waved his Bat-Beer bottle at his phantom orchestra.

He stopped conducting, focused on me, and said, "What do you mean? There won't be any America. There'll be a North American jurisdiction. The whole continent is going to be a melting pot to throw the masses into. You better get with the program. I'm telling you this for your own good, Joe. And forget the American Dream, or they're going to give you your walking papers, and you know what that means, a one-way trip to the vaporizer."

I could see that Chuckles was too far gone; the Bat Beer had done its foul work. He flopped over on his cot, overcome by the kinky brew and with failure.

"You Christians," he mumbled, on his way to dreamland. "And, by the way, aren't you forgetting this is Canada?"

He was right. I was always forgetting this was Canada, but home was where your heart was. And if the Americans weren't able to save themselves from the imminent rule of evil that was rising from their grass roots to destroy their way of life, then I, Joe LaFlam, Christian Detective, albeit Canadian, would have to save them for their own good. And then the American Dream of rags to riches would be preserved and justice for all would prevail, and then any kid growing up, north or south of the border, would be able to stand up proud to be an American.

Chuckles tossed and then turned toward me, his eyes wide open.

"CUT," he yelled, hallucinating in his sleep.

CHAPTER TWENTY-FIVE

We were all lined up in the center-front row for the mid-morning service, listening to Pastor Bernard give a teaching on finances. I wondered now why I had come, other than to buy some time to get a message to Alfred and Abner. Pen and her sisters weren't here, for whatever reason, and my new mom and dad had not yet arrived home from their trip. Pastor Bernard was here, of course, but what was my bond with him? He was only my pastor, and pastors were a strange bunch anyway. They never did anything right. Most of the time they were nosy and controlling, and the rest of the time, when you really needed them, they were uncaring and aloof. To add to their dysfunction, they insisted on trying to involve you, to get you to volunteer for their pet projects. And as if that wasn't enough, they conspired to pry money out of you, as if they had some sort of right to it.

Money. There was the rub. Before I had any, the giving was easy. Ten percent of very little wasn't much. But now, what was I supposed to tithe on? Was I supposed to give ten per cent of the considerable sum my new parents had given me? They were family after all, and they had, no doubt, tithed on that money already. And since I wasn't making any money yet in my business, the money they had given me was going into paying expenses. That meant I was in a deficit position. So, how was I able in good conscience to tithe, when I was going into the hole? You couldn't tithe a deficit. Ten percent of a minus amount was still nothing. Here I was a rich man, but as far as tithing went, my hands were tied.

Pastor Bernard's teaching this morning was emphasizing the importance tithing had on your overall financial health. He said that if you didn't tithe, then God's ten percent that you kept for yourself wouldn't amount to anything anyway, because it really didn't belong to you, it belonged to God. It was His. Following Pastor Bernard's reasoning, if you tithed, you were getting one hundred percent of your income, because that ten percent wasn't yours in the first place. But if you didn't tithe, you were only getting ninety percent of your income, because the other ten percent was wasted and would come to nothing, not being blessed by obedience. So you were a net loser if you didn't tithe.

Warming up to his message, he then addressed the question of whether you were supposed to tithe on your net income or on your gross. Pastor Bernard told us the answer. Your gross, of course, because that was your income. End of story. To me, net, gross, what did it matter? But I resolved to experiment sometime in the future, perhaps giving on my net one month, on my gross the next. That is, when my first income came in.

Since Crusty and Chuckles were with me this morning, I was disappointed the message was on money. As an evangelistic tool, a message on tithing didn't inspire the lost to make a dive for the altar. Church people, of course, had a natural aversion to the topic also. I wondered what message Crusty and Chuckles were hearing.

Crusty leaned into my right ear and whispered, "He's quaintly whacko, isn't he?"

I immediately concluded Pastor Bernard's financial advice was sound, since evil didn't agree with it. But I still didn't feel any release to give.

Then Pastor Bernard told us the score about offerings. They were the amounts you gave above and beyond your tithe. He said offerings from a cheerful heart would be multiplied back to you for Kingdom work.

Again, Crusty whispered into my ear, "Aren't you glad we're eliminating money?"

"Stop that," I said.

"Oh, Joe, they can't hear."

"No, my ear, you're creeping out my ear."

Abner, sitting to my left, said, "Hey, quiet, I'm tryin' to learn here how to stay outta the gutter."

I was beginning to feel convicted. I reasoned that even though I was unable to tithe, since I was running a deficit, in theory I was still able to give an offering directly from my sizeable bank account. But would that do me any good as far as multiplication went, because it wasn't above and beyond my tithe, which I was unable to give? Or was I to give an arbitrary amount and call that my tithe, and then give an offering on top of that? And would God notice? And did God really need my money anyway? And why did these pastor types have so much trouble with their church finances, and why did they feel compelled to lay their failure on the rest of us?

"I'd be tithin', if we were gettin' paid this month," Abner said.

"Right, thank you, Abner, I'll take care of it," I said.

Yes, I would take care of it. But the ones I really needed to take care of were Crusty and Papa and all the rest of them who thought they were better stuff than the average Joe who lived his time and then was nought. Star Stuff thought it could get away with robbing us of death's meaning. If you eliminated the meaning of death, what did anything matter? The vaporizer was as good a way to go as any. But even though it was true we were all goners, it was our eternal destination that was the important thing. Crusty and Papa planned to go to their reward just as stuff, but if I had my theology right, they were, in the end, destined to discover that they had become very hot stuff indeed.

Pastor Bernard concluded his tithing presentation with the comforting assurance that the primary purpose of his teaching was not to increase giving in the church, since we were doing quite nicely thank you, but to lead the congregation, individually and corporately, into continued financial health and prosperity. He admitted, though, that increased income for the church was an obvious by-product. The glum crowd began to stir, as Pastor Bernard dismissed us with a blessing. The worship team played an upbeat departure tune, but nobody was clicking their heels. I wondered who would be the first to inform Pastor Bernard that tithing was a bad subject for a Sunday morning sermon. If you needed a message on the subject, you were better served bringing in an expert, from the outside, an itinerant financial hit-man, and scheduling the meeting on a Saturday or Sunday night, with voluntary attendance for only those interested.

I felt glum, too. Not because of Pastor Bernard's message. There was really nothing I could do about that. I had shaken off my earlier conviction concerning tithing, identifying it as an accusation of guilt shot at me by the enemy of my soul. No, I was glum because I didn't have a plan. The cell phone I'd snatched from my desk was a dud. Dead batteries. And last night I had been left in the loft with only the thoughts in my head for company, and Chuckles, full of Bat Beer, camped in his cot beside me. My only hope this morning was to get a message to Alfred through Pastor Bernard.

"I'm just going to go say goodbye to Pastor Bernard," I said to Crusty.

"That's fair enough," she said.

I was surprised by her willingness to let me go. Evil was funny sometimes. Just when you thought you'd figured evil out, it would trick you and do the unexpected. Like those times when you'd defeat a frontal attack in one area of your life, and then, lo and behold, up another would pop behind your back. You had to be circumspect at all times in the battle against the unseen enemy. I headed toward the altar, where Pastor Bernard came forward to greet me.

"You're still alive," he said. "I'm happy to see you. Last time we talked you were out to save the world."

"Shh," I said, and then I felt convicted for shushing my pastor, but at the same time, I knew I was justified, because some things were more important than respect for his spiritual office.

"What now?" Pastor Bernard said.

"I need you to get a message to Alfred."

"He's been sitting right there with you. Why not tell him yourself?"

"Shh, I can't go into that now. Put your hand on my shoulder and pretend to pray for me."

"Pretend to pray for you? I don't think I should pretend."

"Then pray for me silently, and I'll do the talking, like I'm repenting for not tithing."

"Not tithing? Ever wonder if that's why things aren't going so well for you, Joe?"

"Just pray, will you?"

Pastor Bernard put his hand on my shoulder and bowed his head. I had no way of knowing whether he was praying. "Okay," I said, trying to force a tear or two for effect, "The raid's set for tonight to spring Dano and bust the bunch of them. I'll meet Alfred and Abner at the entrance to the Cave at midnight. Got it?"

"Yes, I've got it," Bernard said.

"By the way," I said, wiping my eyes with a tissue from the box provided, "do you consider yourself an intellectual?"

"Well, I suppose I might fit into that category, yes."

"That's what I thought. You're in double trouble, but I'm here to save you. I won't let you down."

"Thank you, Joe, for being concerned about me."

"Joe LaFlam at your service, Pastor."

"Well, yes, of course, Joe, and thanks for coming this morning."

"Another thing," I said. "There's a woman named Esther in my homegroup."

"Ahh, say no more," Bernard said. "She had an attraction to your father at one time. She wasn't happy when your mother came along."

"How'd she get on the Board?" I said.

"You're in a group with her, and you don't know?"

"Yes, I know," I said. "But did you know she wants to get rid of my dad?"

"And then I'd be next," Bernard said. "Something has to be done. It won't be pleasant. We could lose half the congregation. She's made a lot of friends."

"Why does church have to be so hard?" I said.

"It's the people, Joe. Nobody's perfect. That's why forgiveness is at the heart of our faith."

"I forgive her," I said.

"I do too, but it's going to be a mess anyway," he said.

Pastor Bernard alerted me to the approaching, muffled footsteps, laid down by the dainty feet of evil Crusty.

I said, "Yes, I thoroughly enjoyed your tithing message, Pastor. I won't be able to come any longer, but I do agree your theology is sound in the financial department, and I pray you'll be blessed."

"Coming, Joe?" Crusty said.

"Yes, I'm coming, but before we go let me introduce you to my former Pastor Bernard. Pastor, Crusty, Crusty, Pastor."

Crusty said, "Charmed, I'm sure."

"Are you a believer?" Pastor Bernard said.

"In the stars," Crusty said. "Has Joe told you we are to become one?"

"I was just about to do that," I said, rescuing Pastor.

"We certainly won't be back again, will we, Joe?" Crusty said.

"I'll miss you, Joe," Pastor Bernard said, "and so will the rest of your church family."

"Come along, Joe," Crusty said, "we'll be late for lunch with Papa."

I nodded and winked at Pastor Bernard and then turned down the aisle, evil Crusty on my arm.

I said to Crusty, "I have to say goodbye to Alfred and Abner and, of course, to dear Aunt Margaret."

"Well, hurry up, Joe, and we won't make a sentimental scene, either, will we? We're above all that now."

We approached them at the back table. Abner and Alfred were drinking their coffee; Aunt Margaret sipped a juice.

"I'm going now," I said. "And where I go you cannot follow."

"What do you mean, dear?" Aunt Margaret said.

"They're puttin' him away," Abner said.

"Can it, Abner," Alfred said.

"When are the wedding invitations coming out?" Aunt Margaret said.

"Don't worry," I said. "It will all come clear one day soon."

"Oh, I hope so, dear, especially for your sake," Aunt Margaret said.

I gave her a quick peck on the cheek, offered my hand to Alfred and Abner, which Alfred shook, and turned and marched away, slippery Crusty skipping at my side, and Chuckles bringing up the rear.

Outside, I could see clearly now, the rain had gone. Tonight was the night we were busting out Dano, the time when all the evil schemes of hell were going down, or, in actual fact, coming up.

CHAPTER TWENTY–SIX

I lounged on my futon in my private cave. Lunch had been a sordid feast. Papa gorged, and Crusty, as usual, hid her evil beneath her cheery voice and her thin veneer of pretty skin. I resolved I would not join them for dinner. I would fast, waiting for the midnight hour to toll. Tonight their hides were mine. I stared at the lop-eared bunnies and reflected on evil and our civilization's flimsy coat that cloaked the beast in us all. Lurking beneath that coat was unrepentant evil, its pitchfork eager to poke its victims, setting us on fire to war, like steroidal wrestlers with a tired script.

I bounded to the bat phone and dialed six for the Pods room. It was time to tell Dano when his freedom would arrive.

"Dano here," he said.

"LaFlam, here. We're busting out, midnight tonight."

"And what about our families," Dano said, "are we just going to throw it all away? I don't think so."

"Never mind Papa's threats. They're hollow. We're taking the whole bunch of them down tonight, all of the numbers, especially Papa One and Crusty Seven. As for Chuckles, I'm not sure. He's a funny kind of guy."

"I know. We've shared some Bat Beer together."

"I don't drink," I said. "Oh, sure, maybe at a wedding, you know, a small sip of champagne, or at a birthday party, maybe one cool one, or sometimes wine on an extra special night of dining at an expensive restaurant. That is, if no one's offended."

"So you tried the Bat Beer."

"It didn't agree with me," I said.

"Too bad."

"Be ready."

"Roger."

"Joe," I said.

"Yeah, I know."

I hung up the bat phone. Now, my chore was to wait. And waiting wasn't easy, when the spaces between the ticking of time grew long. And the evening's fast multiplied the length between the spaces, gnawing at the depths of my existence. I had plenty of time to regret not seeing Sissy, to revel in her long black hair, to be absorbed by her piercing yellow eyes, to marvel at her God-given nose, to.... There was no point in going any further. But I did long to tell her the score. I'd failed to keep my promise to let her know my progress, but there hadn't been an opportunity for me to do that, and, besides, all would be forgiven when I returned her Dano to her. I eyed the bat phone once more. I wondered again if they would be listening in. Since I had too much time on my hands, I decided to find out.

I dialed Sissy's number.

"Hello," she said.

"Joe, here," I said.

"Please tell me some good news, Joe," she moaned. "I do need so much to hear some good news for a change."

"I know what you mean. The world's in a terrible mess. Sometimes, I think it would be better not to watch or read any news at all. It's all negative, and that constant barrage of negativity sure doesn't help my negative thoughts one bit. I've heard that some people have just cancelled the paper and thrown their TVs out, end of story...."

Sissy shrieked, "NO, please, my Jake, what about my Jake?"

"Right. That's why I called. We're busting him out tonight, sister."

"Please, call me Sissy. And oh, Joe, I can hardly wait. Please tell me it's so, Joe."

"I just did, tonight at midnight. Now I have to get off this bat phone in case it's bugged."

"You're my hero, Joe."

We hung up, and I hung my head, always the sacrificial hero, never getting the girl. But there was no time for self-pity now, and then I remembered there was plenty of time between now and midnight for self-pity. Why hadn't I said eight, or even seven? What had been so important about midnight? Nothing. Nothing at all. The word "nothing" echoed in my brain, that simple word, which had echoed throughout human history, bringing with its emptiness the thudding hollowness of desperation that searches for something to fill the void. But even if I never, ever got the girl, my void was filled. I'd solved the puzzle. I knew my meaning.

The red light on the silent bat phone flashed. Who was calling me now?

"Joe?" Crusty's voice said. "Are you sure you won't come for dinner?"

"Not tonight. I've lost my appetite. Forgive me."

"Forgive you? We'll work that idiotic concept out of us soon."

"Whatever you say, sister."

"Please, call me…I mean…are you teasing me again, Joe?"

"You know me so well," I said, and winked at nothing.

CHAPTER TWENTY-SEVEN

The bat clock said 11:55 p.m. I was preparing to strike. I'd made my way through the maze of tunnels and found the spiral staircase that led to the Cave nightclub's parking lot. During my ascent, I was aware of the ease of my passage. Stalactites, stalagmites, and bats, all fake, were my only companions. I saw no one, no guards, no evidence of resistance, and that made me uneasy. Was this a trap? Was I leading Alfred and Abner into a life of servitude, or worse? Was that their plan, to ensnare Alfred and Abner, too? I would soon know the answer. And would a positive answer mean that we would be enslaved, or, heaven forbid, that we would be the first ones to die in one of my cases, and therefore make this case, The Case of Twelve, my last? What a loss that would be for the world.

I made it topside. The night air reverberated with the city's confusion, which I rebuked. Then I saw them drive into the lot. They parked and climbed out of a Maserati. I went over for a closer look.

"Didn't you hear Pastor Bernard's message this morning?" I said.

"Are you the only one allowed to drive a nice car?" Abner said.

"Okay, never mind, come on, let's go," I said.

"Where are we going?" Alfred said.

"We're going to spring Dano and blow the whistle on the rest of them, of course. Are you packing heat?"

"Yes, here's your gun," Alfred said. "But have you seen any guards or weapons down there tonight?"

"No, but that doesn't mean there aren't. My guess is they've probably got laser weapons, too. I know for sure they've got a fully functioning hologram theatre. Who knows what else they've got? And, sure, they've got guards. Dano's a guard. He's guarding the pods now."

Alfred said, "What's keeping him here, is it Crusty?"

"No. You don't get it. They've threatened to destroy his family's business if he doesn't cooperate. And a good son wouldn't do that, even an anti-everything son. So there's goodness in Dano, I can tell."

Abner said, "You can't trust those rich folk. Every one of them's a money grubber. Nobody's got no values anymore. Rulin' the world, pilin' up fortunes, for what? I'm storin' up my treasures in heaven from now on, and you'd be best advised to do the same."

Why did Abner have to be right, and make like he was the one who came up with it first, as if I, his mentor, didn't know it already?

"Right now, we're going to find Dano," I said to Abner, "we can talk about our heavenly treasure later."

"Yer the boss," Abner said. "And I'll give ya this much, at least fer a change yer not just sittin' around."

I received Abner's compliment with a nod, and led them across the parking lot and down to the depths of the Cave. I didn't know where to look for Dano, so I picked one of the first tunnels we came to, one I thought I hadn't been down before, though that was difficult to know, since most of the tunnels looked alike. They were basic black, their stalactites glinting in the neon-green fake candle-light. After about twenty yards, a side door came into view. Bingo, there it was. On the door was the word, *PODS*, in black lettering on a green background.

"Pay dirt," I said. "Our man Dano's in there, unless I miss my guess."

I slid open the rock. My eyes adjusted to the white light glaring from florescent tubes, and sure enough, there was Dano, about six feet seven, Kung Fu moustache and all. He was the spitting image of the guy in the Polaroid that reliable Sissy had shown me. She wasn't the kind to let you down. But there was something wrong. From behind the florescent tubes that ran the length of the seven foot pods, two other figures emerged. Were they armed and dangerous? I reached for my piece, and then I stopped. What a providential outcome. There they were, Papa and Crusty, here with Dano, three peas in the Pods room.

I pulled out my piece and said, like McGarrett on a roll, "The jig is up. Papa and Crusty, you're busted. Dano, over here."

"You must be Joe," Dano said. "You do know they're serious about our families losing their fortunes. And they know how to do it, too."

Abner said, "Yer too fixated on money. What do ya want, yer freedom or yer money?"

Crusty said, "Put away that silly gun. What do you suppose you're going to do with it?"

"I'm taking you in. There's got to be a law against all this. By the way, Dano, let me introduce you to my partners. Bell, meet Dano, Dano, Bell."

Crusty said, "Never mind the introductions."

I wasn't taking orders from Crusty anymore, "Booker, Dano, Dano, Booker. Bell, Booker, and LaFlam Detective Agency, at your service."

"Dano has always been free to leave," Papa said. "You, too, Joe, and nothing is going to happen to either of your families."

"Sure, you say that now," I said, "when we've got the drop on you."

"No, we mean it, Joe," Crusty said.

"I don't believe you; you're both coming with us."

"Where to?" Papa said.

"Yes, where to?" Alfred said.

Abner said, "Ya, I'm dyin' to hear."

I said, "We're going to take you to the authorities and tell them what you've been up to here."

"What are we up to?" Papa said.

"Well, you're fixing to take over the world."

"We haven't been altogether honest with you as far as that goes," Crusty said.

"Well," I said, "I do know for sure you're not honest. That's a fact."

Papa looked at Crusty; they both nodded in agreement.

"We're not head Spelunkers, Joe," Crusty said.

"What? What do you mean, you're not. Then what are you?"

"We're a research and development company," Papa said, "specializing in genetic engineering, and also, for one special, preferred client, we do some screening of personnel from time to time."

I lowered my gun.

"Yes, Joe," Crusty said, "I'm afraid I have some bad news for you. You've scored very poorly on our Spelunker aptitude tests. The Spelunkers did have some interest in you, when you recently proved difficult to get rid of, but now we know for certain your survival was only dumb luck. You wouldn't even qualify as a cave doorman. We will have to ask you to go, Joe."

"What about me?" Dano said.

"We would prefer you go, too," Papa said. "We have only been keeping you here for our amusement."

"So, you're not Spelunkers," I said.

"No," Papa said. "We only work for them occasionally. You would never get so close to a head Spelunker as easily as this, would you, Alfred?"

Alfred shook his lowered head.

"But there are Spelunkers, right?" I said. "I mean, they do exist?"

"You have that fact right at least, but they are infinitely smarter than you are, Joe," Papa said.

A terrible thought shot through my mind, like a spear gun arrow streaking through a jellyfish. Did I dare even ask?

"What about Sissy?" I said.

"Have you ever seen us together?" Crusty-Sissy said.

"You mean, there's no Sissy?" I said. "You are diabolical. You're the evil twin twice. But how is that possible? How could you have so much hatred for someone who doesn't exist?"

"That's easy. You liked her way better than me, didn't you, Joe, admit it? Well I'm not her, and I'll never be her. I'm me, and I'm better than she ever would be, if I ever was her again, which I don't intend to be, ever."

I was glad I'd had the wisdom not to get too mixed up with either one of them, though if I had, I still would have preferred Sissy, no contest. But poor Dano; he'd lost in love twice to a different version of the same person. Life was funny that way.

"There's nothing more to be done here," Alfred said.

"Are you coming, Dano?" I said.

"You're sure nothing will happen?" Dano asked Papa and Crusty.

"Positive," Papa said. "The powers that be have assured me of that and have authorized me to pass on the message to you."

"So that's it then," I said.

"That's it," Alfred said.

"'Fraid so," Abner said. "You really busted this case wide open, didn't ya, Mr. Private Eye? Ya found a guy for a client that don't exist. If I were you, I wouldn't hold my breath, waitin' to get paid. I told ya more than once, ya don't trust nobody with yellow eyes."

I was proud of Abner for his clever summary of my current situation. I had struck out once more, but I took some consolation in knowing that I hadn't fallen for evil's deceit. Lust and power were found far from me. I had defeated them, even though, as it turned out, they were a lesser level of evil than I was led to believe. But that didn't matter. I had believed they were a deep evil, and I had resisted. And to discover that I had been rejected by Spelunkers was also a blessing. My low score on their test was confirmation I was not the evil type, and that made me glad. I was not a failure, and my meaning was affirmed once again; yes, my meaning was found far from the evil tunnels of power that ran this planet earth. My meaning was to serve, and serve I would, and as for this case, The Case of Twelve, I considered it solved. Dano had been found, and the sleaze that had brought him under had been partially exposed, maybe not to the world, but to me, and to Alfred and Abner and to anyone else we might tell this sad tale of power and depravity to. I had served my purpose. Yes, service was the key. I decided to add a catch phrase to our yellow pages' listing, and to our sign, and to our business cards, *Detectives Who Care.*

"What about Chuckles?" I said.

"He's well paid," Papa said.

"Well, that's that then," I said. "We'll be going, but don't you, Crusty-Sissy, ever stick your sharp nose into a big time detective's office again."

Crusty said, "Right, Joe, but let me clarify. The powers that be won't touch your families' fortunes for now. But they might make different, less friendly, decisions in the future. So when you're thinking of me late at night, your dear Sissy-me that is, when you're all alone, remember the Spelunkers, Joe, and think about them long and hard until fear begins to drip sweat down your temples. And then when you hear a strange sound, you'll repeatedly ask yourself the same unrelenting question. How safe am I? Yes, think about it, Joe, how safe will you ever be?"

"Hear, hear," Papa said.

"You're finished then?" I said.

"Yes, thank you," Crusty-Sissy said.

"Good," I said. "Then I'm going to remember to pray for you, specifically that your Star Stuff doesn't burn in hell for eternity."

"There's no need to do that, Joe, I'm Presbyterian. To me, this is just a job."

So, she was a sister after all, a twisted sister, on the road to hell, or was she? Well, whichever. I saw no point right now in sorting out the whole issue of predestination.

"Well, adieu," Papa said. "It's been good to know you. We have other fish to fry. We have to keep on top. The competition is fierce in this business."

The four of us left, leaving Papa and her behind, and then, of course, we'd left Chuckles behind, too, wherever he was. I turned as we exited the open rock to see them standing there, the two of them, so alone and needy. But I was unable to help them now. They had made their choice. DNA Research and Development was no easy field. I had some sympathy for their lot in life.

Back up top, Dano told us he was catching a cab. There was no room for him in the Maserati anyway.

"We'll keep in touch," I said.

"Sure," Dano said, "we'll keep in touch, and thanks."

Dano disappeared around the corner, and Alfred flicked his remote at the Maserati.

"Incidentally," Alfred said, "here are your bullets."

"You mean my gun wasn't loaded?" I said.

"We didn't want to have any accidents."

"Ya," Abner said, "and I suppose for the ride back, you'll need to be sittin' on my knee, too."

I reflected on recent events as we sped toward the future, Abner's knees bony and unpredictable. Sure, they'd won this round, but they hadn't seen the last of Joe LaFlam, Christian Detective. No, they wouldn't see the last of me until it was over, and it wouldn't be over until those scum that lined the underbelly of the world were brought to justice. Somewhere the sun was shining, kids were laughing, and apple pie was baking in the oven. No, it wasn't over; it wasn't over until the end.

CHAPTER TWENTY-EIGHT

So the Case of Twelve had wound down to a successful conclusion, or that's the way I liked to look at it. Dano had been rescued, and that was enough. And sure, I hadn't succeeded in returning Dano to my client, because, in fact, my client hadn't existed. And sure, it hadn't turned out the way I expected, and sure, the Spelunkers were still in business, but everyone knew you weren't allowed to pick your endings, because if you were, there would be a lot of confusion over who was head honcho on this planet. We'd all be trying to live like Kings and Queens, but we'd soon discover there weren't enough thrones to go around. Happy endings were scarce, and that's the way life was supposed to be here on terra firma. Not knowing how life might turn out kept us all on the straight and narrow, jockeying for position on life's highway, except of course for those poor souls who couldn't care less.

On the other hand, I and many others like me were in the know. We knew how life turned out; we knew what the ultimate ending was. We'd read the back of the Book, and for a lot of us, that was all we'd read and all we knew, and we lived our lives in that light. We knew there was a happy ending coming for us, when all had been said and done. And why? Because we were saved, that's why. And that's what counted when it came right down to the finish line.

The intercom buzzed.

"There's someone to see you," Pen said.

"Who is it?"

"He says he's one of your group mates."

"Is it George?"

"Yes, he says his name is George."

"I already told you I was expecting him."

"I know."

"Then why didn't you just say, George is here to see you."

"You're the detective."

"Never mind, send him in, and by the way, do you know where Alfred and Abner went?"

"They haven't called in. They're unhappy with you, you know."

"Thank you, I know that, just let me know if they call, can you do that?"

"If they do call, do you want me to interrupt you?"

"No, just take a message."

"As you wish."

Unhappy George came in, his head down, and plunked himself in my client's chair. I empathized. Well, I didn't empathize with him in every way because unlike me he was married and had wife problems. Sure, I had wife problems, but that was because I didn't have one. The two potential wives I had lined up, turned out to be the same deceitful one, and they had only been lined up in the sense that when the case was solved, and my celibacy was ended, then I would have been free to mate, but since Sissy/Crusty had only been a joker in the game, I was left holding a losing hand. And, in that sense, if Al decided to take a powder on George, we would be in the same boat, except he would have at least had his shot at marriage, unlike me, who had never even come close. Again, I had to wonder why.

"Sorry, George, I've been busy with another case," I said.

"That's alright...an' that. Like I told you on the phone, Al says she will be sticking closer to home now."

"Is that so? Well, maybe your worries are over then."

"But she still won't tell me what she's been doing."

"Maybe you should just let sleeping dogs lie, maybe she was having an affair and it all fell through. Maybe the acting thing was only a cover for that. And now she's back and repentant."

I could see my speculations hadn't cheered him up.

"How can I take her back…an' that, when I don't know if she was unfaithful?"

"The fact is there's no way for you to know, if she won't tell you. You'll just have to trust her."

"If she was a committed believer, I would be able to trust her more."

"Why would you?" I said.

"Yeah, I guess you're right."

"Would it help if I spoke to her?" I said.

"Then she'd know I'd been talking to a private detective."

"No, not really, I could introduce myself as one of your home-group brothers."

"Why would she tell you anything?"

"I've got my methods. That's the business I'm in, remember?"

"Would I have to be there?"

"No, I'd approach her at the coffee shop, and tell her I'm concerned about you, ask if she's got time to talk. What do you think?"

"Okay, I guess so. Anything's worth a try. I can't stand not knowing…an' that."

The intercom buzzed. I answered.

"Alfred and Abner are on the line," Pen said.

"I told you I didn't want, oh, never mind, put them on the speaker phone. Alfred? Abner?"

"Oh, you're there," Abner said. "See, Alfred, I told you he'd be there, sittin', taking care of the store."

"I've got a client here, are you coming in today?"

"Do you need help?" Abner said.

"Alfred, are you there?" I said.

"Yes, I'm here. We'll be there in half an hour."

"Thank you."

"See you then," Abner said, and hung up.

"Those are my partners," I said.

"So, you're the boss?" George said.

"Yes, of course, I'm the LaFlam, in Bell, Booker, and LaFlam. LaFlam is at the end, and that means I'm the boss."

"You don't need to have them with you when you talk to her, do you?"

"No, I'm experienced at going it alone. I just came off an important undercover job. That's one reason I haven't been able to focus on Al and your situation. I was going it alone, exposing the bowels of the earth to the light of day. I didn't get down all the way to the bottom dwellers this time, but I did skim some scum."

"Sounds like it was an important mission," George said.

"More important than you know," I said. "The final confrontation hasn't come yet, but it will, and I'll be ready for them. The fate of the whole world is at stake."

"I hope you get to the bottom of it then, when the time comes," George said, "since it affects us all…an' that. But, in the meantime, would you please talk to Al."

CHAPTER TWENTY-NINE

I knew that talking to Al wasn't going to be easy. But my experience with Sissy/Crusty had at least helped me understand how some of these dames ticked, and how their outsides could be pretty but their insides, well, that might be another story. That discovery had changed my wife-requirements. From now on, a woman's outsides didn't have to be that pretty, as long as her insides were nice. So, it was okay if her insides were nicer than her outsides, which I still hoped would be gorgeous, too, but if her insides were exceptional, then it was okay if her outsides were plain, but not homely. Although, different people had different tastes. One person's homely might be another person's heaven, and vice versa. I was pretty sure though she would have to be a Christian, but if she wasn't, then I would have to have a strong sense, using my discernment, that she would be converted at least by the end of the first five years, if we lasted that long being unequally yoked, which, of course, was George and Al's big problem at the moment.

Al was nominal, and that meant she was no Christian at all, which I knew got her off the hook for a lot of things the way the world thought, but not the way we thought, that is, not the way George and I and most of the rest of us committed Christians thought, as we fought to maintain our faith, surrounded as we were by this crazy mixed up world of anything goes.

I headed over to Starbucks, the purring of my Mercedes bringing peace to my soul. I would see what I would see, and if it wasn't pretty, then so be it, but at least I'd have gotten the job done. My hope was that there was a simple, clean explanation for Al's behavior, one that would satisfy George.

Inside Starbucks, the late-morning crowd was in the throes of settling their strings and tuning their invisible vibrators to whatever sound the rest of the day might throw at them. Behind the counter, Al labored to satisfy the masses. Her plainness was appealing. I could see where George might find her attractive to the point of marriage and to the point of jealousy and to the point of divorce, if she were found unfaithful. But maybe he wouldn't be able to make the jump to divorce. Maybe he would forgive her and then make her suffer for her transgression for the rest of her life. No matter, that wasn't my call. I only had to get the goods on her; I didn't have to do the counseling.

I ordered my Chocolate Brownie Frappuccino Venti from Al, paid, took my receipt, and moved aside to wait. A few minutes later, the other gal set my drink on the counter. I saw a soft chair empty by a table at the far corner of the room. I grabbed my Brownie Frappuccino and raced what looked like a Black Grande to the chair. My Frappuccino won. Black coffee steamed away.

I knew that Al's shift was due to end soon. But now that I was here, my confidence had taken a dive. I talked a good game to George, but now that the chips were down, was I going to be able to play my hand? On the plus side, she looked approachable enough. I sucked the straw and waited. I didn't have to wait long. There she went, off with the apron, into the back to get her coat and purse, straighten the plain brown hair, get ready for the street. In a few minutes out she came, in a hurry. I needed to flag her down.

"Excuse me, it's Al, isn't it?" I said.

Al stopped. "How do you know my name? You're the one who drinks the morning Frappies, aren't you?"

"Have you got some time to sit for a minute, I'm a friend of your husband, George, we're in the same homegroup."

"Is there something wrong?"

"No, there's nothing wrong."

Still wary, Al sat down across from me. The light from the windows struck her hair, and she seemed to light up, no longer plain and brown, but attractive, larger than life.

"What are you staring at, if this is...."

"No, nothing like that. I just need to talk to you about George."

"Has something happened? Is he alright? You're not the police?"

"No, I'm not the police; don't let the blue fedora fool you. As far as I know, George doesn't have any problems with the law. No, it's something else. I got to know your husband in our homegroup. You know, where we talk about our lives, and George is having a rough time, and I know this might seem nosy of me, I mean you might ask yourself, like why is this guy sticking his nose in where it doesn't belong? But George is in bad shape, and I'm only here trying to help."

"What do you do at those homegroups, anyway? I've noticed they haven't helped George much."

"It's hard to explain."

"You know, of course, that what you are doing right now is highly suspect, so there better be a really good reason for it, or both you and George are in big trouble."

"Don't get nervous, sister, I'm a professional."

"So, you're a counselor, then?"

"No, I'm a private investigator."

"You mean George has hired a private detective?"

"No, I'm doing it for free. We're groupmates."

"And what does George think he needs a private detective for?"

"It's touchy."

"Okay, I get it. Well, here's a news flash for you. I've been wanting to keep it a secret, but you give me no choice. I've been working at another job to make enough money for a trip back to England this summer to visit George's family. His dad's very sick, and this might be George's last chance to see him."

"You mean you've been starring in porno movies so you can take a holiday in England."

"Porno movies? You're kidding."

"You're not? Then what's Weirdest Name Possible Productions?"

"I can't believe I'm sitting here answering these questions. And I guarantee it will be George who will be answering the questions next. So, my husband has had me followed. If you can't trust your..."

Al choked back a sob.

"Okay, so what is WNPP, then?" I said.

Al recovered and composed herself.

"They've just started to do some work for corporations," she said, "corporate videos, that kind of thing. I got a job as an assistant. I wasn't experienced enough to get a job on screen, not yet, anyway."

So, she was legit. There was no reason not to believe her. And she seemed so nice. I was ashamed of George for even suspecting her. He no doubt needed some serious inner healing.

"Why couldn't I find out anything about WNPP?" I said, stifling a Frappuccino belch.

"I told you, they're new. And that means I'm getting in on the ground floor, and it also means I might have a future with them."

Now that I saw Al here in front of me, I could easily see that she wasn't the porno type. She probably would even make a good Christian someday. I knew I had to try to bail George out.

"George was only trying to protect you and your marriage," I said.

"He has a good heart, but he's so insecure. Are all you Christians insecure?"

"No, some of us are solid, set in stone."

"I've wanted to join him in his faith, but why? It hasn't done him much good that I can see. He got converted after we were married. We had fun before. Now, in his spare time, he mostly just reads his Bible and prays."

"Good for George," I said. What else could I say?

So there it was; George was a bad witness. Why did we spend

so much of our time being bad witnesses to our faith? There George was, so insecure he thought his good wife was a porno queen. And here I was ready to burn Al at the stake for no reason other than my brother was hurting. What was the matter with us all? Sure, the Church started with the Truth, but what happened after that? It took a few thousand years of history to produce the middle-class Church in America. Sure, the Church was effective in China, and sure, there were Christians being martyred all around the world, but that didn't help us here. We were all on course down easy street, and later we'd all be raptured before anything bad happened, leaving the unsaved folks to fry. There was so much wrong with the Church, why did I bother? Why? Because it was the only game in town, that's why. At least I knew that for sure. And when you were in the know, you knew, and that's all there was to the story.

"Why are you all so…so…different?" Al said.

"If you knew, you would know," I said.

"I'd like to know, but I don't."

I didn't know what to tell her.

"Why don't you come to Church?" I said.

"Is that the answer, going to Church?"

"Well, no, not exactly," I said.

"What then?"

"Hasn't George told you?"

"About Jesus?" Al said.

"Yeah, that's it," I said, relieved. I was getting better at this evangelism thing. "Ask him some more about it."

"When I'm talking to him again, I might."

Al calmed again and became reflective.

"I went to Sunday School when I was a kid," she said.

"I thought your parents were hippies," I said

"Yes, but they weren't strict orthodox hippies. My mother belonged to a church when she was a kid, before, you know, the love thing, and then later she sent me there, too."

So, it was true; Al had confessed to me with her own mouth. She was a closet nominal Christian.

"Don't be too hard on George," I said. "His heart's in the right place."

"I know," she said, "or I wouldn't have married him."

Al then sprang to her feet and said, "I've got to go and catch my bus. This has been educational. Thanks and goodbye." She hurried out without looking back.

So, there it was. Case solved. Al had been working a secret legitimate gig, to earn money to take George to England. Things were looking good for George and Al. I felt confident they had the possibility of a great future together, and they would have an even better one after Al got herself saved. I could see she was headed in that direction now, since I'd had my little talk with her. And she thanked me, too. Yes, I'd succeeded in my mission, unless, of course, she was lying through her teeth.

CHAPTER THIRTY

The whole gang was at homegroup. I told an anxious George over donuts and Coke that in my professional opinion, his missus was clean, and, for reasons that would become clear at a later date, I wasn't permitted to explain the whole situation to him now, but he would just have to take my word for it. He responded by saying he had weathered well her threats to kill him, if he ever did anything like that again. I resisted reassuring him that nobody ever died in my cases. But George was still concerned that she would never tell him the big secret, and then he would never know. On the other hand, he was content to have escaped with his life. I told him again that Al would tell him the truth soon, and then he began to cheer up, and hope began to rise in his face, as we took our seats for our evening's growth in church community. I decided not to test fate—though as a Christian, I didn't believe in fate—by asking him if he had a sick dad in England. I only hoped Al wasn't lying through her teeth.

"Icebreaker!" Esther said, elated.

Phil and Mary exchanged glances, no doubt puzzled, since Esther had recently nixed icebreakers. But Esther seemed to be in a different mood tonight, a happier one, almost ecstatic. I wondered what was up with her, and whether her plot to overthrow my dad was still in the works.

"If you were a pastor, what kind of pastor would you be?" Esther said, too happy for words.

She was hitting below the belt now. I knew this had to be for my benefit. I wondered what our meeting would be like without her. It only took one bad apple to spoil your homegroup barrel.

Husband Bill got the nod from Esther and said, "If I were a pastor, I would be the kind of pastor who was always on the job, meeting the needs of my flock."

George, his joy increasing, said, "If I were a pastor, I would be an expert in marriage counseling, and I would bring healing to all the married couples in my church…an' that."

"I can't really focus on this," Phil said.

So, that was a surprise. Phil had decided to rebel against Esther's authority.

"Me either," Mary said.

Good for Mary and good for Phil, I thought. Esther's good cheer sagged. It was my turn.

"If I were a pastor," I said. "I would be the kind of pastor who would eliminate all manipulation and control from my church."

"Hmm…I'm impressed," Esther said.

That was surprising; Esther seemed to mean what she said. So, there it was. She thought she was a mighty Kingdom warrior, and was unaware of her own methods.

"Why are you impressed?" I said.

"I thought you were short on understanding, what with your private detective inefficiencies and all. The apple doesn't fall too far from the tree."

"He solved *my* case," George said, defending my ability.

"He did?" Esther said

"Congratulations, Joe," Phil said.

"No porno movies, then?" Bill said.

"No, not likely," George sputtered at Bill.

"That's right, she's clean," I said. "It was all a misunderstanding."

"Should we talk about it, George?" Esther said.

"Okay, you're right," George said. "I guess I got carried away with jealousy and lack of trust, not knowing what she was doing… an' that."

"And what was she doing?" Esther said.

"Well, I don't know yet," George said. "She won't tell me, it's still a secret...an' that, but Joe says she's innocent, and he's the private detective, so that's good enough for me."

"So, she still might be making porno movies?" Bill said.

"No," George said, "I already told you."

I hoped Al hadn't been lying through her teeth.

"So your trust issues were dealt with, then." Phil said.

"Yes," George said. "I'm trusting that Al and Joe are trustworthy. Joe's a Christian brother, and I should trust him, and Al's my wife, so I should trust her, even though she's only a nominal Christian."

"But we do know that a nominal Christian is no Christian at all," Bill said.

"Nominal or not," George said, "she's still my wife."

"I'm sure your trust is well founded," Esther said.

"She seems like a good person to me," I said.

"Scripture says nobody's good, no not one," Bill said, "let alone someone who's nominal."

"So," Phil said. "Let's move on, the ice seems to be broken for now."

Esther said, "I'm not done. I didn't even have a turn."

"Okay," Phil said, "what kind of pastor...?"

"I can do it myself," Esther said. "If I was a pastor, which isn't entirely out of the question, I would be the kind of pastor who hears directly from God and then perseveres to accomplish God's vision, no matter who stands in the way, or what anyone says."

Well, at least she was being honest about it.

"You've got a pipeline to God?" Phil said. Phil was getting annoyed.

"Don't you think it would be wise for a pastor to confirm her vision with other people," Mary said, "other people who also hear from God, and have proven wisdom and character?"

"No," Esther said, "that's simply an excuse never to get anything done."

"I never felt good about women being pastors," George said.

Esther and Mary glared at George.

"You what?" Esther said.

"The trouble is," George said, "I haven't always been a Charismatic, and the church I went to before didn't ordain women."

Esther and Mary looked to Bill and Phil.

"Oh, sure, I'm fine with it," Phil said. "It goes without saying."

"It's crazy even to discuss such a thing," Bill said.

I was staying out of it.

"Yeah, but," George said, "what about the part where women are told to learn in silence, and aren't supposed to boss men around?"

Esther began to steam, but Mary only shook her head, like she was feeling sorry for George.

"Talk about mother issues," Esther said. "That just shows you what's the matter with our current senior pastor. He can't even establish firm doctrine in the church so everyone knows where we stand. How are we supposed to move forward if there are young men in our midst who don't recognize legitimate authority? We might be Charismatics, but we don't have to be loosey-goosey."

"Why are you always calling my dad down?" I said.

"I happen to know," Phil said to Esther, "that our senior pastor does believe that women are equal as far as ministry goes."

"But does he know what he's doing?" Esther said.

"And he's hardly ever around," Bill said.

"I don't think we should be talking about our pastor this way," Mary said.

"Bernard is more suited to the job," Esther said, "he's younger and he's got a lot more enthusiasm and energy."

"I didn't want to bring it up before," Mary said, "but I didn't care for you binding retirement to our pastor last meeting."

I was proud of Mary. She was pastor material, not Esther. I wasn't totally sure where I stood on women pastors. I sort of took them for granted. But I knew where I stood on Esther. She wasn't one. I made a mental note to establish a theological position on women in pastoral ministry, in case Alfred and Abner ever came up with such a question.

"Some on the Board are unhappy," Bill said.

Esther glared at Bill. He'd let the cat out of the bag. So, there was a coup afoot, but was Bernard in on it? Time would tell. As for right now, I knew I needed to make a conscious decision to love Esther and Bill despite their plotting. They might yet be diverted from their course of destruction.

"I'm telling my dad," I said.

"Oh, he knows already, I'm sure," Esther said.

"How would he?" I said.

"He would if he checks his e-mail when he's out of town, on those trips he takes, partying with his new wife."

So, with my dad away, Esther had been inciting an uprising, and now she was no longer hiding her intentions.

"I wonder," George said, submerged in his own speculations, "if Al would care, one way or the other, about what I thought of women pastors."

"Don't worry," Bill said. "Nominal Christians don't have theological positions."

So, the fix was in. There was no question about that now. Esther was going to take a shot at splitting the Church of the Manifest Presence. And why? Because Esther wasn't happy. And when Esther wasn't happy, nobody was going to be happy. You only had to look at Bill. How many Esthers in how many churches in this great land of ours weren't happy? And those were just the Esthers. What about the men? They were even more skilled at causing splits than women. They'd had more practice. I sure hoped Bernard wasn't in on it.

"So you're going to split the church?" I said to Esther.

"No, you wouldn't!" Phil said.

"That can't be!" Mary said.

"Is that the detective talking?" Esther said. "And, besides, we're not splitting the church, that's a negative term. We're going to set the church free to fulfill her destiny, and those who oppose us, well, what they choose to do, that's up to them."

"Is Bernard in on it?" I said.

"We'll see, won't we?" Esther said.

"We'll see," Bill said, milking glee from Esther's coattails.

"Yes, I was born for such a time as this," Esther said.

We were going to have a time alright, whether it was going to be Esther's or not was debatable.

"I think," Phil said, "under the circumstances, we'd better adjourn our group for this evening."

"Yes, exactly," Mary said.

"As you wish," Esther said, "you're the leaders, for now. Come, Bill."

Esther and Bill left, their mission accomplished. But why had Esther made her play tonight? Was Esther's whole act for my benefit? Yes, the devil loved to act. Maybe she wanted to draw a line in the sand in front of me, to make sure the message got through loud and clear, so that I would pass on to my dad how bold and confident of victory she was. Was it an act of intimidation? Who knew? But what I did know was that Esther and Bill were on a one-way trip to nowhere. It might take a while for them to get there, but unless there was divine intervention they would, sooner or later, find themselves out in the cold with no return ticket.

"I'm sorry this had to happen," Phil said to me, "especially since you're so new here and the pastor's your dad."

"Yes," Mary said, "but don't worry, we'll put a notice in the bulletin. I'm sure there are other brothers and sisters who will be happy to be part of our little group. But, we have had some trouble keeping people. I don't know why."

"Maybe Esther and Bill will change their minds," I said, attempting to encourage Mary.

"No, not now, not after she was so bold," Phil said. "She won't change her mind. It's too late now."

Mary said, "It's never too late, is it? I wouldn't like to think it was ever too late."

"Don't let it bother you," Phil said.

"But it does," Mary said. "Think of my friends at the Club."

"You know you shouldn't do that, Mary," Phil said. "You'll only get depressed."

To reassure us, Mary said, "But he doesn't mean clinically depressed. I'm only sad about it once in a while."

"That's right, you're doing fine, honey," Phil said.

Mary said, "Do you think there's a possibility that we might spend too much time focusing on ourselves?"

"Of course not," Phil said, "what else would we do?"

Continuing to dwell in his own space and time, George said, "Do you think Al will ever tell me what she's been doing?"

"Sure she will, George, sure she will," I said. "Or my name's not Joe LaFlam."

And then I hoped, once again, that Al wasn't lying through her teeth.

CHAPTER THIRTY-ONE

My penthouse office was peaceful this autumn morning, as I waited for Alfred and Abner to make their appearance. Summer had come and gone since we'd rescued Dano. Business had been slow and the church scene quiet. It was like the devil had taken time off for bad behavior, or maybe people were just too hot in the summer to cause much trouble. Either way, I wasn't worried. I expected business to pick up later in the fall season. On the home front, Aunt Margaret and the rest of the family had been curious to know what had happened to Crusty and our plan to get married. I saw no reason to share the whole story with them yet. I reasoned there would be some better time in the future to go into the details. To his credit, Pastor Bernard had been understanding and had suppressed his natural curiosity, but Aunt Margaret had been the most persistent and, I thought, the most determined to be irritating. I was nearly forced to move out, but my immediate need for stability outweighed the burden of enduring her compulsion to bless me with her piercing insights. After a month or so, her comments—about my profession and my inability to get hitched—waned. And my working life and my church life again had settled into the plodding norm.

I knew that Pastor Bernard over the last few months had only received the odd mild rebuke from some of the more well-to-do for his unfortunate tithing message. The majority had accepted the teaching and seemed to be prospering as a result. Alfred and Abner said they were reaping the benefits of their obedience already, and were in full agreement with Pastor Bernard. I hoped soon I would be able to join them, so that I might be guaranteed the future security of a blessed financial life.

There were still unanswered questions that continued to haunt me about the Case of Twelve, even though the Spelunkers and their ilk were nowhere to be seen. And our family's fortune remained intact, so we were safe for now. Yet, there were questions this autumn morning, spinning through my mind, as they often did, questions that needed to be answered, questions that had confounded me over the long hot summer. The central question, of course, was why did Papa and Sissy-Crusty go to so much trouble? Why did they spin so many lies? Why did they bother to lead me through their whole song and dance? Was it just so they could screen me for Spelunker membership? No, that was too simple. There had to be more to it. There was a part of the puzzle still missing. But where to look? There must have been something I missed. A loose thread somewhere. This is what made the detective business so compelling and, I hoped sooner or later, so satisfying. You had to follow the clues until the obvious was discovered, and it might even be found right under your nose, too. But what was it?

Interrupting my deliberations, Alfred and Abner stormed through my custom mahogany door.

"Man, I sure looked younger on TV," Abner said, "skinnier, too. Why was that?"

"You looked just fine," Alfred said.

"So did you," Abner said. "I'll have to admit."

Abner turned from his discussion with Alfred to say, "Look, surprise, surprise, he's just sittin' there. Who would have guessed?"

"What's going on?" I said. "Have you been talking to the news media? Is it the Spelunkers again?"

Alfred and Abner sat down.

"No," Alfred said.

"Well, what then?" I said.

"Yer a star," Abner said. "There's no other way to explain it. Yer a star, made of real Star Stuff."

"Star Stuff?"

"Yes," Alfred said. "You made it to the big time. Last night, on TV, you were the star of a new reality show, *Super Dupers*. Their season opener was all about you."

"Ya," Abner said, "it was yer night to shine."

"I haven't been on any reality show," I said.

"Are ya sure?" Abner said.

"Yeah, I'm sure," I said.

Was I sure? Hmm. I leaned back in my rich, big-city detective's chair and reflected, staring out my big-city detective's office window. The dots began to connect one after the other. A few scenes from earlier events began to pass before my eyes and then string together, with a beginning, a middle, and an end. Ahh, yes, the case was finally solved. How diabolical. Yes, the missing pieces of the puzzle had come home to roost. And it wasn't a pretty picture.

"Ya made fools of us all," Abner said. "How could ya fall for all that Star Stuff, and that initiation ritual, and mixin' yer genes, and *Networks of Joy*, and all that tripe?"

Alfred said, "Chuckles, as it turns out, is a talented director."

"Private Eye and Chuckles, swillin' Bat Beer," Abner said. "That was a precious scene. It'll be all over church."

"Sorry," Alfred said. "But I did try to tell you that something smelled bad about the whole thing."

I felt dizzy. The revelation of my stardom was too heavy a burden for me to carry. The room began to spin around, but then after a few rotations the room slowed and came to a halt, and I regained my focus. The shock had left as fast as it came. I knew that it was at times like this that a man proved himself, and I wouldn't disappoint myself now. I was bigger than the Spelunkers, and all those who would try to put a good man down. I had to hang in there. I had to persevere for the good of all. I was a detective first and foremost, with a good future in the business. I was a darn good detective, at the top of my game, and I knew my meaning besides. Then I realized I had won. In the face of adversity and ridicule, I had conquered my negative attitude syndrome. If being a fool for America on a reality show wasn't able to defeat me, then I was able to handle anything. But I felt a hint of anger rising up from within me, too—righteous anger, of course—and it needed to be released in order to bring closure. The outlet for it was clear. They would have to pay. That was the American way. Duping me with deceitful reality was one thing, but they would have to pay for the privilege. Their insidious hides were mine. Making them pay was more than an obligation; it was my duty to make them pay. Now that my mettle had been tested again by the Spelunkers, and I had absorbed the blow, I was even more dedicated to the American way. And even though I was a Canadian, I knew what I had to do.

"I can sue, can't I? They didn't have my permission. I didn't sign a release form."

"Sue?" Alfred said. "Have you forgotten about the Spelunkers? They don't like being sued, and they don't like you, and don't forget they own most of the media. You sue, you lose."

Abner said, "And ya had to drag us down with ya."

"And Dano, what about Dano, was he in on it?" I said.

"In on it?" Abner said. "He'll be up for an Emmy for best supportin' role in a reality show."

And then there was darling Sissy-Crusty. She was good, real good, and headed for stardom. An incorrigible actress, and no doubt *Super Dupers* had been her big break. There was no question about it; she was good. And no, she wasn't evil; she was following her American Dream. I'd known all along she had a redeemable quality. She was Presbyterian after all. And to her it was only a job. Nothing personal. Maybe she was available now to get together and talk over our time on the show. I thought I might offer her a few reflections, compliment her on her performance, ask to watch the outtakes with her, and enjoy a laugh or two at my own expense. And what about that Chuckles, a director, and that scar of his, only makeup; I was glad of that, and Crusty's nose and her yellow eyes, all fake. Yes, Hollywood was filled with talented professionals.

"Do you think they might pay residuals?" I said.

"No chance," Alfred said.

"That reminds me," Abner said. "*If* we're gettin' paid this month, we should be gettin' a bonus for humiliation."

"I'll take care of it," I said. "Do you think I can get a tape of the show?"

"Ya don't get it do ya?" Abner said.

"Sure, I get it, Abner. It's a tough world out there, and we all need something to keep us going, something to spur us on so that we have the courage to show up for work every day. Well I know who I am, and what my purpose is, which is more than most people can say. So I'm content, Abner, I'm content to wait for my next client and see how I can help her, or him, cope with this crazy, mixed up world."

Alfred said, "Every scam artist in North America will be beating a path to our door."

"I'm gettin' me a disguise, and changin' my name," Abner said. The intercom buzzed.

"Aunt Margaret on line one," Pen said.

I picked up. "You should have told me," Aunt Margaret said, excited. "No wonder you were behaving so mysteriously. You kept it for a surprise. I didn't see it, but I hear you were wonderful, dear. Just wonderful. You must have missed your calling. Do you think you might be on again?"

"No."

"Oh, too bad, dear. But maybe another opportunity will come along soon."

"Yes, maybe, see you at dinner," I said.

I beeped her, and the intercom buzzed again. "A Mr. Smith on line one," Pen said.

I picked up. Papa's voice said, "Enjoy the show?"

"I haven't seen it yet, but Alfred and Abner seem to think you presented an accurate portrayal of me and my agency. Do you think you could send me a copy?"

"It's the least I could do," Papa said. "Have your people talk to my people."

So, there was some goodness in Papa after all.

"But while I have you on the line," Papa said, "some friends of ours, if you know what I mean, want me to let you know that the score isn't settled. They did find it amusing to kick-start your TV career and at the same time destroy your credibility should you try to expose them in the future. But if you do decide against all odds to undertake such a foolish course again, remember that your family's fortune still hangs in the balance. Have you got that?"

"Is this for next week's show?" I said.

"No," Papa said, "this is for real. See you at the movies."

Papa beeped me off. I was relieved in a way that the fiends bent on taking over the world were harder to apprehend than Papa and Crusty had been. I now had the hope of future encounters with the Spelunkers, and we would see who got the last laugh. I was relieved, too, that my sleuthing ability was still intact, since I'd had my doubts about Papa and Crusty from the beginning. Well, there it was. Evil endured. It had gone to ground, but still it lurked. It was down there somewhere, in the world, shifting around, preparing to shake the earth with the Big One. But I was here, on duty, Alfred and Abner at my side.

"Who was that?" Alfred said.

"Oh, just Papa asking if I'd seen the show, and...."

The intercom buzzed again.

"Pastor Bernard on line one," Pen said. "We're popular today, aren't we?"

I picked up.

"It's okay, Joe," Pastor Bernard said. "We all make mistakes."

"I know."

"You're taking it well then?" he said.

"Sure, why wouldn't I? I'm a mature Christian, and I know my purpose in life. What more could a guy ask for? Well, on second thought, a wife would be an asset, but besides that, I'm doing fine. I'm flattered really, a Canadian detective making it big on American TV, just like a prime-time American detective. A guy like me can take a lot of pride in having entertained America, if only for one night. What could be better than that, except, as I just mentioned, also having a wife? So, things have never been better. And, as you probably know, nobody died in the Case of Twelve either. And to top it off, I came out of the whole deal secure financially, and, incidentally, I do intend to tithe at some point, just not now. I'd like to make an honest contribution, from my own hard-earned money, if you see what I mean, that is, when I make some."

"I see," Pastor Bernard said. "I'm happy you're doing so well, Joe. See you Sunday then?"

"I'll be there, Pastor."

"I'm proud of you, Joe," Pastor Bernard said.

"It was nothing. You know what they say, a trial's not a trial unless it's a trial."

"Who said that? It was Chuckles, wasn't it?"

"So that part was in it, too?" I said.

"Yes, I think so. It almost sounded scriptural."

"That's what I thought. Maybe you could try and find it."

"I'll look into it."

"Thanks, Pastor."

Pastor Bernard hung up, and the intercom buzzed again. What a day!

Pen said, "A Ms. Taylor is here to see you."

"That's fine, send her in."

The door opened, and, yes, Ms. Taylor had the appearance of just the right case. But for that matter, every case from now on had the potential to be a case for the ages. And whoever Ms. Taylor was, and whatever her case turned out to be, I knew she'd come to the right place. Yes, there was no getting around it. I was good, real good. I was good the way a detective could be good, plying his trade the way I was in this none too perfect world, filled with the flotsam and jetsam of humanity, somewhere in the Pacific Northwest. And I knew now I was destined to see it all, not that I hadn't seen plenty already, but there was plenty more for me to see, and time to see it in, if the Lord delayed His coming. And that was one thing I did know for sure. Nobody knew when He was coming back, not even those wise cracker theologians, so I was in good company there, or bad company, depending on which theologians they were and what particular views you held. Sure, there were crackpots from time to time who predicted the day and hour, but they were doomed in the long run to the quicksand of time. Time. I also knew I had a lot of time to redeem before His return. Too much time, not enough intriguing cases. Yes, the case was the thing. And I could hardly wait for the next chase to begin. I needed to sink my teeth into a tough case, a case that would test me and try me, a case that would make me a better human being. Cases were trials, and how you followed the trail, how you measured up, how you hung in there, were more important than where you ended up. Of course, you were heading to heaven, your ultimate destination, but for now, you were only concerned about your earthly one. That said, she was coming now, gliding, in a floor-length gown, like a princess, taking hidden, tiny steps, her chin elevated and level. She was blonde, elegant, and statuesque. Yes, she had the bearing of a lovely new case to me. Alfred and Abner exchanged glances, and shook their heads.

"You know what they say," Alfred said to Abner. "You can't cheat an honest man."

"Ya, life's a real adventure alright," Abner said. "Let's leave him to it."

Alfred and Abner showed themselves out, and the intercom buzzed again.

"Not now," I said to Pen. "Please sit down, Ms. Taylor."

"It's urgent," Pen said. "Line one."

"Okay, fine, excuse me, Ms. Taylor, I'll be with you in a moment."

It was George. "I'm pretty busy right now," I said.

"Busy, don't talk to me about busy…an' that," George said, yelling and angry. "Fine brother you turned out to be."

"What now?" I said, eager to get on with my new case.

"What do you mean, what now? You know, what now. You were with her the whole time. You were even thinking of marrying her, in a perverted sort of way…an' that."

"Who?"

"Do you think I'm stupid? I saw you on TV…an' that, you spending all that time with Al, playing me along, and now you're playing dumb. I'm coming down there, and you won't like what I'm going to do when I get there."

The penny dropped. Beholding demure Ms. Taylor posing there, I dismissed a foolish thought about quitting the business altogether. After all, I'd only been guilty of a minor error in discernment. And to my credit, I did have an odd feeling about her at Starbucks that last time. Maybe if I'd seen her run. Anyway, there was no harm done. I would explain my position to George and he would understand. So, Al/Sissy/Crusty had been playing me for a sucker the whole time. She *was* lying through her teeth. And no wonder she couldn't tell George. The Spelunkers no doubt had sworn her to secrecy. But poor George, his wife a Spelunker hireling, and a Presbyterian, and a nominal one at that. But at least she wasn't a porno queen. I liked her better with the nose though. I took a deep breath in George's ear, and knew I had some explaining to do.

"I'm celibate, you know, George."

Ms. Taylor raised an eyebrow.

"…an' that," George said.

THE END

RECIPE FOR
LAFLAMBURGER CLASSIC

Makes 4 servings (or one)

1 large onion (diced)
5 Tbs. vinegar (Joe uses malt or apple cider)
Combine in a small bowl.

6 – 8 red potatoes, peeled and cut bite-sized
Place in a large pot of cold, salted water over medium-high heat. Bring to a boil and cook until tender (about 15 minutes). Drain, reserving ½ cup of the water. Pearl the potatoes by placing a dish-towel over the pot.

1 ½ Lbs. of lean ground beef
Brown in a large skillet.

4 Tbs. fake-gravy
(Joe uses Bisto, but any fake-gravy brand will do)
2 cups water (boiled)
Whisk to combine fake gravy and water.
Add the ½ cup reserved potato water to the ground beef. Bring ingredients to a boil. Then add the prepared fake-gravy. Allow mixture to thicken.

To serve, gently nudge the potatoes into a large bowl, pour the simmering hamburger and gravy mixture over the potatoes, and top off with the onions and vinegar. Salt and pepper to taste.

www.ingramcontent.com/pod-product-compliance
Lightning Source LLC
Chambersburg PA
CBHW072233170626
46813CB00003B/1195